the last hiccup

A NOVEL

THe LAST HiCCuP

CHRISTOPHER MEADES

Published by ECW Press
2120 Queen Street East, Suite 200, Toronto, Ontario, Canada M4E 1E2
416-694-3348 / info@ecwpress.com

LIBRARY AND ARCHIVES CANADA CATALOGUING IN PUBLICATION

Meades, Christopher
The last hiccup / Christopher Meades.

ISBN 978-1-55022-973-8
ALSO ISSUED AS: 978-1-77090-226-8 (PDF); 978-1-77090-227-5 (EPUB)

1. Title.

PS8626.E234L38 2012   C813'.6   C2011-906950-4

Editor for the press: Jennifer Hale
Cover design: Dave Gee
Typesetting: Troy Cunningham
Printing: Webcom   1   2   3   4   5

The publication of *The Last Hiccup* has been generously supported by the Canada Council
for the Arts which last year invested $20.1 million in writing and publishing throughout
Canada, and by the Ontario Arts Council, an agency of the Government of Ontario. We
also acknowledge the financial support of the Government of Canada through the Canada
Book Fund for our publishing activities, and the contribution of the Government of Ontario
through the Ontario Book Publishing Tax Credit. The marketing of this book was made
possible with the support of the Ontario Media Development Corporation.

 Canada Council   Conseil des Arts   Canada   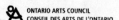 ONTARIO ARTS COUNCIL
for the Arts   du Canada   CONSEIL DES ARTS DE L'ONTARIO

PRINTED AND BOUND IN CANADA

 FSC
www.fsc.org
FSC® C004071

MIX
Paper from
responsible sources

 ANCIENT FOREST ™
FRIENDLY

To Hanna

thank you

Wendy Meades for (still) supporting the dream, for baking me Smarties cookies and helping me revise the ending of this book. Wendy believed that I could become a published author long before I ever believed it and I never could have written this novel without her encouragement and support.

Hanna and Claire, my two little girls. Daddy loves you . . . now seriously, try to be good.

Jen Hale, my editor, took a true leap of faith in signing up this novel on spec. Jen changed my life a few years ago when she picked *The Three Fates of Henrik Nordmark* out of a pile of hopeful manuscripts and decided to work with me. I will forever be grateful and in her debt.

The staff at ECW. Without their hard work and dedication to publishing emerging Canadian authors, this book would still be an MS Word file on a disc in a drawer under considerable layers of dust.

Brian "Bear" Simmers, my best friend of 20 years and (at minimum) the fourth person I would save if the zombie apocalypse were to come this week.

Jamie Rothney, a true friend, for his enthusiasm and encouragement.

Nicole Harvie Simmers, Vancouver's style guru, for being a trusted confidante all these years. Not often is your best friend's wife also one of your very best friends, but in this case it's true.

Joan Witty and Anne Craig for taking care of my mom when she needed you most.

Margaret Helsdon, my mother-in-law, for her boundless encouragement and her tireless promotion of *The Three Fates of Henrik Nordmark*.

Nick Komick and Ann Mariscak for always having my back.

My dad, Larry Meades, for his timely advice.

My first readers: Christina Sielsky Adams, Angela Kruger, and Steve Mason.

My cousins: Traci Meades, Brian Craig, Katherine Craig, Nance Craig, Will daSilva, Joanne Witty-Knox, Derek Knox, Michael Craig, Ellie Vitello, Scott Meades, Sandra Witty, and last but certainly not least, Jim Witty.

During the writing of *The Last Hiccup*, my mother, Susan Meades, lost a brave battle with pancreatic cancer. Mom, I love you, the girls miss you more than you could ever know and I wish you could have lived another 30 years.

Part
ONe

Russia, 1929

They first appeared unexpectedly on Vladimir's eighth birthday, following the swift consumption of three bottles of soda. Young Vlad stood from his seat and leaned over his birthday cake to blow out the candles. He prepared himself with a moment of quiet, positioned his arms on either side of the table, then, instead of blowing outward, Vladimir accidentally and tragically inhaled a long, deep breath. What emerged next was the mixture of a whistle blowing and a frog's ribbit. Vladimir's mother, Ilga, was the first to express shock. "Vladdy," she said in their native Russian, "what a sound you've made." Vladimir smiled and went to blow out the candles when the sound materialized a second time. His friends giggled and snickered in good fun. Then it reared its head again. And again. Like a metronome, the sound repeated at intervals of 3.7 seconds.

Vladimir's mother pulled him aside. "What's wrong, Vladdy?" she said. "Are you sick?" Vladimir shook his head. He felt fine. He just had the hiccups. His mother sent him back to play with the others and kept a close eye on him. An hour later, when Vladimir's condition had still not improved, Ilga sent his friends home early. She sat her son down and looked him straight in the eye.

"Boo!"

The boy just stared at her. He didn't bat an eye.

"Boo!" she shrieked this time and threw her hands in the air.

Vladimir continued to look straight forward, not the least bit startled. After a half dozen failed attempts, Ilga forced the boy to drink a tall glass of water. Vladimir gulped it down, hiccupping several times during its consumption. The water had no effect. In fact, none of his mother's efforts had any effect. For two hours, she attempted every trick she could possibly imagine, from feeding the boy spoonfuls of peanut butter to having him stand on his head and recite the alphabet. By bedtime, she'd completely run out of ideas. "Go to sleep now," Ilga said. "Things will be better in the morning." Vladimir's mother tucked her son into bed, kissed him on the forehead, then shut his bedroom door and lingered outside. *Hiccup.* There it was, quietly through the door. *Hiccup.* It sounded again. Ilga shook her head in frustration, walked to her room and poured herself a stiff glass of vodka. She shot it down in one gulp, rolled into bed and dozed off gently, her son's hiccups forgotten.

When she awoke the next morning, Ilga made herself a cup of tea before waking Vladimir. It was his first day back at school after the winter holiday and Vladimir had a long walk in steep snow ahead of him. "Vladdy," she called down the hall. "It's time for school." When he didn't respond, Ilga marched down the corridor and opened the door to his room. Vladimir was lying on his back in the exact position she'd left him last night. His eyes were wide open. He hadn't slept.

Hiccup. "Good morning," he said. *Hiccup.*

"Vladdy!" His mother ran to his side. "Did you sleep at all last night?"

"No, Mother," he said between convulsions.

Ilga was beside herself. "Well, that's still no reason for you to stay home from class."

Vladimir's mother dressed her son, forced him to eat some bread and marmalade, then helped him with his boots and wrapped him in his winter coat before pushing him outside into the waist-deep snowdrifts. He walked the half hour to school, hiccupping his way through the cold.

As Vladimir entered the school's courtyard, out of the corner of his eye he spotted his classmate Ileana Berezovsky in all her glory. For two years now, young Vlad had been infatuated with Ileana. He didn't really know why. He was still at an age where he detested girls, after all. Like any eight-year-old boy, Vladimir would much rather dissect a squirrel or kick a football through a sealed glass window than engage a girl his own age in conversation. But Ileana was different. A pretty little girl in a sailor suit, she had long blond hair that reached the small of her back; the profile of her closed lips was enchanting and pure. Ileana smelled of sweet cherries and emitted a laugh so intoxicating it stole the very light from the room. Young Vlad could have written volumes on the joy her laughter brought him. He had never actually spoken to Ileana, however. Vladimir preferred to worship her from afar, even when she allowed another boy to carry her books to school. On this day, Vladimir could barely manage a glance at the angelic girl, so heavy was the tired miasma in his mind.

He trudged into the town's schoolhouse, a small building consisting of a classroom and an office. The office was inhabited by the schoolteacher Urie Kochuokova, a giant bear of a man with a quick temper and a firm, almost secular regard for formality and rules. Kochuokova's iron fist was ever-present. Talking out of turn, failure to enunciate a subject-verb agreement in a sentence before the class and often talking too loudly (even when it was a child's turn to speak) were all reasons for Kochuokova to draw forth the wooden paddle that sat in the drawer under his desk. He required all students to refer to him as Professor even though no diploma hung on his wall and he had been educated in the third-smallest township in the country. On the day Vladimir arrived with the hiccups, the Professor was already in a state of ill temperament.

Young Vlad took his seat at the center of the classroom and tried to stifle himself. He held his hands to his mouth and stared straight ahead, deadening his hiccups slightly, but not suppressing them entirely. As the day's lesson in mathematics began, the sound of a dog yelping emanated from behind Vladimir's closed cheeks.

The Professor shot a commanding glare across the room. "What is that?" he said.

Vladimir hiccupped again.

"What is that noise?" The Professor threw his chalk against the blackboard. It sounded again. "I demand to know who's doing this."

Vladimir's face turned red. He could hold his breath no longer. In a torrid burst of air and saliva, young Vlad pulled his hands from his mouth and expelled the loudest yelp yet.

Kochuokova stormed toward his desk. "Is this you, Vladimir? Are you making these noises?"

"Yes, Professor." He hiccupped again.

"We're in the middle of a lesson. I demand you stop this nonsense."

"But I can't."

"What do you mean you can't?"

"I just can't."

Urie Kochuokova scratched his bald head and twisted his jaw in frustration. *I could be in Moscow exchanging pleasantries with dignitaries right now*, he thought. He made as though he were about to walk away, then turned suddenly.

"Boo!" he screamed.

The large man marched forward until he was nose to nose with the child.

Vladimir didn't flinch. His pupils didn't even dilate.

The Professor hovered momentarily, then stood upright. Vladimir could see the thick wiry hairs pulse in Kochuokova's nose. He straightened his jacket, replaced his dangling time-piece back in his pocket and walked to the front of the class. "Back to your arithmetic, children," he said.

Vladimir hiccupped all the way through the day. The Professor's lessons, those stringently regimented lectures Kochuokova had committed to memory, fell into disarray toward the end. He could barely even hear himself think over the repetitive yelping. Like a pack of carnivorous wolves, the students sensed weakness and started to misbehave as the day went on. Talking erupted in pockets with giggling fits interspersing the afternoon. Just before the final bell, a young troublemaker named Pavel Discarov shot a spitball at the back of Vladimir's head. Young Vlad, dizzy and tired from lack of sleep, could only turn around and give him a desperate look. The Discarov boy seemed to sympathize for a moment, then changed his mind and ruthlessly hit Vladimir between the eyes with another wet, tepid wad of paper. Vladimir spent the rest of the afternoon facedown, his hiccups reverberating off his desk.

As the bell sounded, the Professor asked Vladimir to stay behind. The other children ran off to play, all except Ileana

Berezovsky. She walked up to Vladimir and placed a consoling hand on his shoulder. Up close, Ileana smelled like caramel and peaches outside on a clear spring day. Vladimir breathed in a long, deep breath. It was more enthralling than he could have imagined.

"Are you unwell?" Ileana said.

Young Vlad was about to answer when Pavel Discarov called to Ileana from the doorway. Holding her books, he appeared anxious to leave. "I hope you feel better," she said and removed her hand from his shoulder. Vladimir watched her leave, his skin still warm from her touch. The girl's sweet scent filled the air long after she left. Young Vlad would have lingered in that moment for an eternity; he would have basked in its sympathy, its simplicity, the glory of her touch — had not a set of heavy footsteps sounded behind him. Kochuokova stormed up to his side and suddenly Vladimir found himself alone with this mammoth man. He gazed up at the towering figure. The Professor did not look pleased.

Vladimir searched the man's hands for that thick wooden paddle.

Kochuokova scribbled down some words on a piece of paper. "You are not permitted to come to class until your condition betters itself," he said. "Take this note home to your mother. You may come back when you stop making that infernal noise."

"But what if it never stops?" Vladimir said.

"Don't be silly, boy. These things have a way of running their course," the Professor said. He glanced away momentarily and when he looked back, Vladimir had on his face such a look of distress, Urie Kochuokova realized that he alone would have to comfort the lad. Instantly, he regretted taking this job. Thirty-three years ago, his mother (God rest her soul) had declared him gifted. She said he had a way with people, that her little Urie was born to do great things. He had in him the inherent ability to become the next Russian ambassador to any number of great nations: noted, respected, even feared. Now her son stood in this cold room alone with a pale, yelping child. "There, there, boy. Don't sob. It's undignified," he said. "You will be fine within a week's time. Consider this an extended vacation."

With those words, he ushered Vladimir out the door and into the cold.

Young Vlad would never see the inside of the schoolhouse again.

two

Two days later, after several sleepless nights for her son, Ilga herself was exhausted. She had tried every trick from every old wives' tale in her repertoire, each to no avail. Vladimir's hiccups stayed at the same interval of 3.7 seconds the entire time, never speeding up and never slowing down. Ilga poured herself a cup of tea, added a dab of honey and a shot of Kubanskaya, and then approached Vladimir in the living room, where he was drawing in his schoolbook. She leaned over his shoulder and was horrified by what she saw. Instead of the rural scenes and ponies young Vlad would usually draw, he'd constructed a graveyard with his oiled chalk sticks. The nighttime scene was replete with dark birds, scattered corpses and tipped-over gravestones. In the center was a mysterious man, his face broad and sinister. Beside him a skeleton stood half the size of the man. Above this cadaver, Vladimir had spelled out his own name.

With panic in her eyes, her hands shaking, Ilga grabbed Vladimir by the collar of his shirt and dragged him to the front door. "Some exercise will do you good," she said. Ilga forced the boy into his boots and coat. Vladimir looked up with tired eyes that were red from secret crying. Ilga, herself almost in tears, placed her hand square on his back and, with all the force she could muster, pushed him out the door. Vladimir took exactly six paces in the snow before wavering. His left leg wobbled first, then his shoulders hunched forward. There was a single moment in which Ilga thought the boy was going to right himself. "Please, Vladdy," she whispered under her breath. "You can do this." That moment, however — so brief, so fleeting and so hopeful — was only a deceit. In one swift motion, Vladimir fell forward and planted his face in the snow. Ilga shrieked out loud and ran outside in her bare feet. She rolled her son over. *Hiccup. Hiccup.* Young Vlad was too exhausted to speak.

"I'm taking you to the doctor," Ilga said. "I don't care how much it costs. We'll fix you."

Three hours later, Ilga and Vladimir, dressed in their very best attire, arrived by automobile in Igarka, a sawmill and timber-exporting port along the Yenisey River that, though larger than their village, had only recently been granted township status. The car Ilga drove belonged to their neighbor. Unsympathetic to Ilga's plight, he had forced her to barter for use of the vehicle. The two haggled for several tense minutes before eventually settling on the cost of three full bags of flour. Normally Ilga would have balked at such a steep asking price, but she had no other resort.

As she and Vladimir sat in the doctor's crowded waiting room, Ilga looked in her purse. Her son's health care was supposed to be paid for by the state. Officially that was the policy. But local doctors routinely charged additional fees for arranging appointments. This far north, the system was unregulated. Ilga had just enough money to cover one appointment, no more. Vladimir's father, a military man pressed into service in a foreign country, would not be sending back any more funds for at least three months. This was their only chance.

The doctor entered the waiting room. "What's that noise?" he said. An older man with gray hair and failing eyesight, he had popped his head in to speak to the receptionist and was visibly disturbed by the yelping sound. The receptionist pointed to Vladimir, sandwiched between his mother and an elderly lady suffering from the gout. As if to announce that he was indeed the culprit, young Vlad let out the loudest hiccup yet. "Bring the boy in first," the doctor said, effecting an audible groan from the other patients who'd been waiting longer. The elderly lady beside Vladimir did not groan, however. When he was called into the office, she was so overjoyed that she gave Vladimir a little push to help him on his way. The elderly lady let out a slight chuckle, one that would turn out to be her last, as eleven days later she would succumb to a combination of food poisoning and uranium exposure unrelated to the gout.

"How long have you been making that noise?" the doctor said. He was going through his usual list in his physical examination of the boy. He checked Vladimir's heartbeat, looked in his ears and searched the boy's hair for lice.

Vladimir's mother answered for him. "It's been several days now. He can't sleep. Look at the lines around his eyes."

The doctor squinted heavily to inspect the dark puddles of skin that had formed under the boy's eyes. He removed his stethoscope, sat back in his chair and shook his head. "There's nothing I can do medically in this case," he said.

"Nothing?!" Ilga exclaimed.

"Nothing. The boy has the hiccups. That's all. Have you tried scaring him?"

"Yes."

"Hmmm." The doctor rubbed his chin. Suddenly, in one surprise motion, he leapt from his seat, lunged at Vladimir and yelled "Boo!" at the top of his lungs. Vladimir didn't flinch. His eyes didn't even close. He only stared back at the doctor with the same look of confusion, wonder and helplessness.

Having overexerted himself, the doctor lowered carefully

back into his seat. "Have you tried having the boy stand on his head and recite the alphabet?"

"Yes."

"Did you have him recite it backward?"

"What difference would that make?" Ilga said.

The doctor opened a file folder and made some notes, then stood up from his chair. "Bring the boy back in one week's time. We'll see if he's stopped making the noise by then."

Vladimir's mother was nearing her wit's end. "But I can't afford another visit. The trip here cost us dearly. Is there nothing you can do?"

The doctor reached into his pocket and produced the thickest, widest pair of bifocals Ilga had ever seen. He placed them squarely on his nose, reached out and playfully tousled Vladimir's hair. "You needn't worry," he said. "In all my years I've never seen a case of the hiccups that lasted more than a few hours, let alone a few days. This will pass, I assure you."

"What if it doesn't?"

"If it doesn't, come back in a week's time. My cousin Sergei is a renowned physician from Moscow. He's coming to town for a wedding next week. If your boy still presents the same symptoms, I'll make sure Sergei sees him."

"What about the appointment fee?"

"Tut-tut," the doctor said as he walked them to the door. "If the hiccups last another week, payment will not be necessary. Sergei will want to see this for himself."

Exactly one week later, Ilga and Vladimir returned to the doctor's office. When the doctor entered the examination room, he was shocked by the boy's appearance. Vladimir's skin had turned alarmingly pale since the last time he saw him. His eyes were darker and more world-weary. He seemed to have lost weight and, surprisingly, a few bald patches were scattered atop his head. Vladimir had still not slept. The doctor was met with the same frog-like yelp emanating from the boy's mouth every 3.7 seconds.

"My God," the doctor said under his breath. Even without his thick-rimmed glasses, he could see the boy's condition was dire. When he put his glasses on, he became instantly worried that young Vladimir would die from exhaustion before the day was over. "Sergei!" the doctor called out the door. "Sergei, you must come have a look!"

A few moments passed before the three of them were joined by one Sergei Namestikov. Nearly two decades younger than his cousin, Sergei was a strong, broad-shouldered man in his early forties with a full head of hair and a confident white smile. He didn't seem the least bit startled by Vladimir's appearance. Instead, he introduced himself first to Ilga, took her hand and placed a kiss on her wrist. Instantly smitten, Ilga did a partial curtsy the likes of which she hadn't performed since she was a little girl. Sergei closed his eyes and listened to the sounds emanating from the boy. He used his wristwatch to time them. Sergei crouched down, looked Vladimir in the eye and spoke softly. "How long have you been making this sound?"

"Over a week, sir."

"It's been almost two weeks," Ilga said.

Sergei stayed focused on Vladimir. "Does it hurt when you hiccup?" he said.

"No."

"Do you feel any different than you did before the hiccups started?"

"I can't remember what it was like before."

Sergei examined Vladimir's head. "How did his hair fall out?"

Ilga looked at the ground when she answered. "He pulled it out himself at night."

"In frustration because he couldn't sleep?"

Ilga nodded.

"Has anyone tried scaring the boy?"

"Yes." Ilga stroked Vladimir's head with her hand. "Many have tried. It has no effect."

Sergei placed his hand to the tip of his nose and stood in absolute silence. Sergei's cousin, Ilga and Vladimir could each have taken turns counting to thirty during the time Sergei spent pondering the child's symptoms. Finally he pulled his cousin aside for a brief consultation. When he returned, his diagnosis was grave. "The boy will die within a week's time if he does not receive proper care."

Ilga broke into tears. The examination room filled with her wailing. Young Vlad, for his part, stood entirely still, exhibiting no emotion as the hiccups continued. Sergei had fully expected the boy's mother to start crying. He waited for her to calm down, then spoke. "Madam, the boy has singultus — hiccups in layman's terms. It's caused by pressure to the phrenic nerve. This, I'm afraid, is the most advanced case I've ever seen. There is a chance he can still live and be cured. We need to admit Vladimir to the hospital here in Igarka so he can get some sleep. Once he's suitably rested, if the hiccups do not abate on their own, I would like to take Vladimir to Moscow with me. There, at my hospital, my colleagues and I can get to the bottom of this."

"Does he have to go away?"

Sergei stepped closer and took her hand. His eyes penetrated Ilga's. "I'm afraid so. Do we have your permission?"

"Yes," Ilga cried. "Anything to save my Vladdy."

That night Vladimir was taken to the local infirmary. There was no hospital to speak of. Igarka's infirmary consisted of three ramshackle rooms and a single nurse in a rundown shanty behind a sawmill on the pier jutting out into the Yenisey River. One could actually see the chilling flow of water and fragments of ice bobbing under the gaps in the floorboards. Vladimir was placed on a sanitary mattress and given a dosage of morphine one and a half times the recommended amount for a boy his size. Sergei and Ilga watched as the drug took effect. First the boy's expression grew drowsy. Then his limbs fell limp, followed by his eyes slowly shutting. The hiccups, which up until this moment had steadfastly maintained their regular interval, suddenly paused. Three-point-seven seconds passed and there was no sound. Then it was four seconds and then five. Ilga looked to Sergei as though he'd cured her boy. She was about to leap into his arms and express her boundless gratitude when, at the 7.4-second mark, the hiccups returned. They hadn't stopped. Only one hiccup had been missed. Incredibly, Vladimir continued to hiccup in his sleep.

Sergei looked over at Ilga with a somber expression on his face. "It appears the situation is more dire than I first imagined."

Later that evening, Ilga signed a release form over to Sergei for Vladimir's treatment. At 4 a.m., she was sent home to rest.

When Ilga returned to the infirmary the next day she discovered an empty bed where Vladimir had been sleeping. Fearing the worst, she asked the nurse if her son had passed away during the night. The nurse informed her that Vladimir was still alive. He had been taken to Moscow for treatment. Ilga looked out the window and into the endless fields of snow heading west. Tears streaked down her cheeks.

Ilga reached into her purse and pulled out a flask of partially distilled vodka. She took a swift swig and then another. Ilga looked down at the phial. She lifted it to her mouth and consumed the rest in six successive gulps. Vladimir's mother wavered on her feet. She felt the Earth start to slip beneath her and reached her hand out for the windowsill — a terrified, panicked grasp of five fingers consolidating into nothingness — but missed and collapsed in a heap on the floor.

Her son was gone.

three

The initial attempts to cure Vladimir involved subjecting him to a series of sudden terrors, each more horrific than the last, in an effort to scare the hiccups out of him. A snake was brought in and placed at the boy's bedside. Next, several hospital workers dressed up as ghosts and surprised the boy as he slept. Eventually, Sergei commissioned an aspiring father/daughter circus-clown duo at a steep, almost extravagant price to cackle demonically as they chased Vladimir through the courtyard in the middle of the night. All attempts failed.

The boy, it appeared, was quite fearless.

After consulting his staff, Sergei decided that it had been presumptuous to try to stop the hiccups altogether. Instead, he made it his mission to slow them down. To begin with, they established that the hiccups were indeed repeating at an interval of 3.7 seconds. Once this was accepted as fact, Sergei ordered the boy to be hooked up to a machine to monitor his convulsions. A curriculum of heavy medication followed. Each day after the drugs were administered, Sergei's assistants would crowd around Vladimir to scrutinize the duration, intensity and volume of each involuntary yelp. Except for the one hiccup Vladimir skipped when he entered the rapid eye movement portion of sleep, there was absolutely no change in his condition. The interval didn't change. The sound didn't change. And the minor tremor it caused in Vladimir's young body did not change. After months of trying, Sergei's team was forced back to the drawing board.

In the subsequent months, several other theories were put to the test. First, an attempt was made to subject Vladimir to periods of extreme hot and cold. Not only did this undertaking meet with abject failure, but it resulted in both second-degree burns on the child's right leg and the loss of Vladimir's left middle toe to frostbite. Next, steps were taken to induce vomiting in the boy, the notion being that Vladimir could not continue to hiccup were he busy expelling food and water through his mouth. This process proved to be both too messy and too difficult to quantify. Quickly abandoned, it was followed closely by the administration of electroshock therapy. Notes weren't taken during these sessions and few details were made public, but the results were clear — the hiccups had not abated and a mishap during the third treatment resulted in the attending physician losing partial movement in his arms. Electric shock was never again attempted on the boy.

On suspicion that Vladimir might be experiencing an allergic reaction to his surroundings, the decision was made to sanitize his environment. A small, sterile room was painstakingly prepared. First, all furniture was removed. Second, the window overlooking the courtyard was boarded up. The floor was scrubbed, cleaned and disinfected, all of the walls fitted with thick, anti-allergen plastic. Finally, the light bulbs were removed from their fixtures. Two attendants placed the boy inside this dark room with only a sound transmitter and then sealed the door by boarding it up as they left. An hour passed with Sergei's team listening to Vladimir hiccup through an intercom. Then a second hour went by. It did not look promising. Finally, at the eleven-hour mark, the hiccups started to grow faint. Forty-three minutes later they stopped altogether. A great cheer erupted amongst the hospital staff. Doctors embraced nurses. Strangers shook hands. Congratulations were declared. The celebration spread down the hall to where Vladimir's fellow patients launched into a voracious rendition of the Russian national anthem. Sergei found himself so caught up in the excitement he even allowed two of his coworkers to raise him on their shoulders.

Only Ilvana Strekov, a flat-chested, mouse-like nurse's aide with a history of pilfering her relatives' glass figurines and an almost debilitating narcoleptic affliction, hesitated in joining the merriment. She walked up to the sealed door and placed her hands on the boards. "Doctor?" she said.

Sergei didn't respond.

"Doctor?"

Sergei had just been lowered down by the jubilant revelers and was shaking hands with the hospital administrator when he saw Ilvana. "Yes, my dear?"

"How is the boy able to breathe in that room?"

Sergei stopped dead in his tracks. His expression morphed from joy to bewilderment to shock and then fear all in one fluid motion. "Get him out of there!" he bellowed. Nearly a hundred faces turned and stared blankly at Sergei. "I said get the boy out! He can't breathe!" Sergei pried at the boards with his hands. Quickly the maintenance crew leapt into action. Within seconds the boards were removed and the protective seal was slashed open. Sergei opened the door and ran to Vladimir. The boy wasn't breathing. Sergei started performing mouth-to-mouth. "Stand back! Give the boy air!" He pounded on Vladimir's chest in between breaths. "Live, damn it, live!"

★ ✳ ★

The next morning, on a day of thick, driving rain, Sergei met with his colleagues in the hospital's conference room. The faces of those assembled were characterized by dejection. Yes, the boy was still alive. Sergei had just barely managed to resuscitate him. But the hiccups remained. Sergei stood up from behind a mountainous stack of papers. "Everything we've done so far, every attempt we've made, has been to no avail," he said. In a sudden, unexpected fury, he threw the case file in the air, scattering pages around the room. "We've spent almost an entire year treating this boy and still he suffers. Still he must be put to sleep with drugs. Still he hiccups. Collected here are fourteen of the most gifted medical minds in all of Russia. Surely we must be able to solve this mystery. Does anyone have anything new to add?"

A single hand shot up.

"Yes?"

"Perhaps we could replace the patient's phrenic nerve with a man-made device. Or a transplanted nerve from a recently deceased patient."

"No." Sergei shook his head. "We would be stretching ourselves too far if we entered the delicate arena of nerve replacement. Anyone else?"

In the corner, a short, nondescript physician, thirty years of age with tortoise-shell glasses and an eager expression on his face, stood up. Having long allowed his wife to write his research papers for him, he'd snuck into this meeting uninvited alongside one of his more esteemed peers. All week he'd prepared for this moment. Were his suggestion to be accepted amiably, he would no longer have to carry with him the overriding, unstoppable awareness that he was a fraud. He spoke with all the courage he could muster.

"Perhaps we should step back and think about this case from a metaphysical point of view," he said. "Has anyone considered that the hiccups might be the boy's soul gasping to get out of his body?"

Sergei shot the man a look so full of violent, disgusted disregard that the others in the room shuddered. "If I was in the military," he said, "I would have you shot." He leaned on the table, clearly exasperated. "Does anyone have an intelligent suggestion?"

In the front row, directly across from Sergei, the shoulder of one Alexander Afiniganov began to roll in a forward motion. Alexander, whose long-standing rivalry with Sergei had earned him the unofficial designation as Sergei's nemesis, was the most brilliant doctor in all of Moscow. Ever since grade school, when Alexander's diorama depicting the directional flow of molten lava had bested Sergei's cross-pollination of plants in a junior achievement science fair, no matter what success Sergei achieved, Alexander had managed to eclipse him. In every facet of life, Alexander always stayed a nose ahead. When Sergei finished second in his high school class, Alexander finished first. When Sergei was permitted entrance into the most prestigious university in all of Russia, Alexander accepted a full scholarship to study at one of the world's oldest and most respected institutions in London. In medical school, while Sergei was busy composing a paper on anxiety disorders, Alexander beat him to publication with an exemplary dissertation on the combined effects of triskaidekaphobia and coulrophobia.

Alexander was a better chess player.

His ice hockey team routinely defeated Sergei's.

Even in love, Alexander always managed to win. The day

after Sergei announced his engagement to a beautiful, kind woman with a big heart and a healthy dowry, Alexander made public his engagement to one Natasha Krilsolov, a slightly more beautiful woman with the heart of a saint and an overwhelming, almost outlandish patrimony endowment. Years later, after the two men had been assigned as senior residents at the same hospital and Sergei was reaching the end stages of a bitter and at times devastating divorce, Alexander had informed him, with an almost gleeful look in his eye, that his wife, Natasha, had died suddenly in an unfortunate ice-fishing accident, leaving Alexander the bulk of her estate and what could only be described as a harem of potential young brides.

In each instance, Sergei would watch as Alexander's shoulder began to roll. Slowly at first, the ball of his shoulder churned forward. Alexander would crack his neck to the side and then quicken the pace. Standing at the front of the conference room, Sergei watched Alexander grind his shoulder. It could mean only one thing — Alexander knew something about his patient that Sergei did not.

"Yes, Alexander?"

Half of Sergei wanted to grab his nemesis by the throat and shake him until he stopped. The other half couldn't wait to hear what he said. Vladimir was Sergei's prized patient — he had long protected the boy from the other senior residents. Were he to cure this boy's hiccups, the presentation of his research would receive an ocean of accolades. Despite his worry that he might lose Vladimir to his archrival, Sergei stepped to the side and encouraged Alexander to speak in front of the group. Alexander did stand up, all confidence and deserved bravado, churning his shoulder in front of everyone. He reached a single hand up to the widow's peak where his hair met his forehead and then adjusted his round metallic glasses. A hush fell over the others as his powerful baritone filled the room.

"You have all been involved in treating this boy. You have attacked his hiccups with heat and cold, with sudden fright and the deprivation of oxygen. You attack and attack and attack, all the while failing to understand that you are combating the symptoms, not the root cause of his ailment. If you have a gash on your arm and you place a towel on it, does it stop the flow of blood? Sometimes, yes. But what if the blood does not stop? You can apply the towel a hundred times to the same wound and still it will bleed. It is only when you go beneath the surface to find the severed artery that you can rationally decide on a prudent course of treatment.

"I urge you to stop wasting your time on these futile attempts at halting this patient's hiccups. Instead, you must discover why this is happening. Find the cause of his convulsions. Flush it out by any means necessary. Then, my dear colleagues, you may return to your attacks, only with focus and purpose."

The room fell suddenly silent. All eyes were on Sergei. Even Alexander, who rarely looked his rival in the face, waited on Sergei's reaction with bated breath. Sergei rubbed his chin pensively, something he often did to buy time when he'd already made up his mind but wanted others to think he was in the process of coming to a rather difficult decision. His rivalry with Alexander was a thing of local legend. For years it had been well documented in both hospital gossip and, surprisingly, a feature story in a state-run newspaper. Many of those assembled today had witnessed a physical confrontation between the two doctors last year in the cafeteria in which, following a pointed exchange of words, a plate of turnips had been smashed, several punches had been thrown and threats of further violence had been uttered. The general consensus was that Sergei would bristle at his adversary's proposition. Sergei, however, knew better than to dismiss Alexander out of spite. With one simple analogy, Alexander had distilled Vladimir's dilemma to its core. All this time Sergei had been treating the symptom, not the disease.

Sergei swallowed hard a mixture of saliva and pride. "It appears I've needed your help all along, old friend." He offered his hand to Alexander. "Shall we work on this together?"

Alexander, who was neither Sergei's friend nor in the practice of helping others, surprised himself by accepting his rival's handshake. And, despite his skepticism, he agreed to help. "Together we will cure this boy."

A smile formed on Sergei's face. "Then let's get started. We have a great deal of work to do."

four

Initially, Sergei and Alexander's working relationship was professional, at times bordering on courteous. All those years of animosity had fostered a mutual tolerance for each other's skills as physicians. They got along so effortlessly at first that their tolerance morphed into something resembling respect. Their first order of business was to make a detailed list of all ailments that might be afflicting Vladimir. A rigorous testing schedule was arranged and they began examining the boy for signs of the following illnesses — scurvy, rickets, guinea worm pestilence, shingles, gonorrhea, the Egyptian plague, gravidity, whooping cough and, finally, the common cold.

The boy was poked at, prodded and pricked with needles. His blood was taken so many times that the nurses eventually had difficulty finding an unspoiled vein each time more tests needed to be run. On two separate occasions he was made to endure a lumbar puncture. His glucose level was checked. The roots of his hair were examined under suspicion he was succumbing to advanced aging syndrome. Through it all, Vladimir never complained once. He endured tubes sliding down his throat, spinal taps and enemas with a sedate pragmatism far beyond his years; his attitude owed partly to his obedient nature and partly to the aftereffects of the drugs that kept him asleep at night. He was simply too exhausted to complain.

After five long months of tests, Alexander approached

Sergei while he was strolling down the cobblestone path between the hospital's main building and the mental health ward. This trail was lined with the most beautiful trees in all of Russia. They stood seven times taller than a man, and their branches reached over the heads of passersby. Even the perpetual winter could not disturb the landscape's beauty. The crisp white blanket of snow had crystallized the branches, leaving the trail protected by thousands of dangling icicles.

"It appears there is nothing physically wrong with the boy," Alexander said.

"So you're telling me there's nothing we can do?" Sergei stared straight down and followed a set of footprints in the snow.

"I'm not suggesting we should abandon all hope."

"Then what exactly are you suggesting?"

The two men were being coated by a light, languid fall of snow. Alexander found it infuriating. Sergei considered it the most peaceful feeling in the whole world.

"Have you considered that Vladimir's condition might stem from something other than a physical ailment?" Alexander said.

Sergei kept walking. That possibility had always been in the back of his mind. Late at night as he lay awake recollecting the timeline of the escalating injustices his ex-wife had incurred upon him, Sergei would often consider the idea that young Vladimir was indeed quite mad.

Alexander continued. "I'm not suggesting that he's somehow fashioned this illness in his clever little brain or that he's experiencing some kind of psychosis. I haven't yet identified all the factors at play, but there's something unique happening here. I'm starting to believe there is a battle raging in the young boy's soul — a battle between his conscience and his most base impulses, between the seraph and the devil's sprite, between good and evil."

Sergei stopped in the snow. Strangely preoccupied, he hadn't quite heard what Alexander said. Even now, as his rival kept talking, all Sergei could focus on was how he suddenly felt far too warm in his large scarf and fur hat. He shook his head slowly, then looked at the ground. This snow hadn't been touched since it fell. A blank sheet of paper lay out before him and Sergei could write anything on it he wished. He ignored Alexander and stood mesmerized by the pure white glory.

Alexander took two long strides into Sergei's line of vision; he dragged his feet across the blank page and sullied Sergei's inner peace in the process. "Have you listened to a word I've said?"

Sergei was so lost in thought, he'd only picked up fragments of words fluttering in the air. Finally he looked up from the snow and was met by Alexander's frustrated expression. *What has he been going on about? It's no matter*, Sergei decided. He knew what Alexander must be getting at.

"I will handle this." Sergei pushed past his rival and turned off the path to head down a snowy slope. Alexander watched from the cobblestone as Sergei marched off into the distant courtyard.

Sergei removed his fur hat and ran his fingers through his hair. He'd been preparing for this for weeks, even months now. It was only as Alexander blathered on about God knows what that he decided to accept the truth. The possibility was no longer remote. If Vladimir was to be saved, it had to be confronted directly.

"The poor boy," Sergei said to himself. "He may very well be insane."

five

The next day Vladimir was transferred from the hospital's main wing to the mental health ward. An attendant carried the heavily sedated boy along the same snow-covered cobblestone path where the doctors had taken their walk. Sergei could hardly bear to watch them remove his patient. He stood at his office window, partially shielding his eyes, partially looking straight on in defiance as young Vlad was taken through the front doors of the psychiatric unit. Secretly Sergei feared that Vladimir might not make it out of that building alive.

During the course of Sergei's residency, the mental health ward had been the least organized, worst funded and most chaotic department in the entire hospital. Patients, some of whom were severely demented and quite dangerous, were allowed to roam the halls free of supervision. Violent incidents in that ward were nearly a hundred times more common than in the main building. Several times when the drugs used to sedate the lunatics were in short supply, the inhabitants had attempted a coup against the hospital staff. Outnumbering their captors thirty to one, the patients had the means to overtake the ward. Yet they could never manage to organize themselves well enough. Inevitably, each fracas would end with a single inmate screaming in frustration over the inability of the others to complete even the simplest of tasks. After all, how difficult is it to behead a nurse? Sergei shook his head. The hospital simply did not have the funds to properly equip or staff the building. He said a silent prayer for Vladimir, then left for the night, hoping to find the boy alive tomorrow.

When Sergei arrived at work the next morning, Vladimir had already been returned to his bed in the main wing. Apparently, the sound of his hiccupping had caused an uproar in the asylum. The inmates, even those who had no history of violence, became enraged when Vladimir would not stop yelping. A chair was thrown through a glass partition. Next a garbage can was set on fire. This was followed by young Vladimir being stuffed headfirst into a second garbage can. Several of the schizophrenics were planning to light Vladimir on fire. Severely outnumbered, the hospital staff were powerless to intervene. Mere moments before he was set ablaze, the boy was saved by a rogue faction of patients, some who believed his hiccupping was a communication from God and others who appreciated the pure musicality of the noise. A full-blown violent conflict erupted. When it was finally over and Vladimir had been rescued, a number of the victors declared him their divine savior while others simply wanted to dance to his beat. In total, there were eleven broken limbs, seven critical injuries, one beheaded nurse and a litany of damages totaling the equivalent of the mental health ward's annual budget.

Sergei rushed to Vladimir's bedside in the main wing to find the child sitting cross-legged on a cement floor besieged with nonsensical chalk scribblings and a large drawing of a hangman's noose. Deep in concentration, the boy was intently focused on a piece of twine he was twirling in the air. Bruised, chafed and fatigued, Vladimir had a long scrape along his forehead. He still wore the bright blue hospital gown the psychiatric unit used to distinguish its patients from the sane green-robed patients in the main ward. Ragged burn marks ran up the side of his gown while fragments of its hem and sleeves were singed off entirely. Vladimir's bare feet were covered in soot, his legs stained charcoal gray. Otherwise, he was undamaged.

Sergei sat down on Vladimir's bed and took a long look at the boy. He wondered — had Vladimir been scarred by this incident? Would this be the one defining experience that would perpetually plague his patient's dreams or had it just been another unspeakable torment in a long list of unspeakable torments the boy had been forced to endure? Sergei could glean nothing from Vladimir's expression. It was at once stoic, inquisitive, apathetic and haunted by despair. Close to three minutes had passed and still his patient hadn't acknowledged that Sergei was in the room. Young Vlad needed his help now more than ever. Sergei had failed him too many times. He failed in curing him of the hiccups. He failed by allowing Alexander to subject the boy to a random series of painful, invasive tests, each more unnecessary than the last. And finally he failed the boy by exiling him to a land of lunatics solely because he couldn't decide what else to do with him. Sergei brought his hands up to his face and rubbed his eyes hard.

"Vladimir?" he said.

The child's eyes remained fixated on the spinning twine.

"Would you like to go on a field trip?"

Young Vlad looked up and, for the first time since Sergei could remember, the boy smiled.

Two hours later the doctor and his patient were on the other side of Moscow, sitting in a windowless room lined by hundreds of old, unopened books. After his night in the asylum,

Sergei ordered Vladimir to be bathed, clothed and deloused (although not necessarily in that order), and with his combed hair and hospital-provided dress attire he now looked like any other normal child. The only indications of his condition were his abnormally pale skin, a macabre reddening about his eyes and, of course, the persistent, inexhaustible hiccups.

Vladimir reached over to the stack of books resting between him and Sergei on the plump leather sofa. The first was a medical textbook, the second a history of witchcraft. The third one, which Vladimir opened and flipped through with interest, was a graphic, picture-laden account of human mating practices in antediluvian Europe.

"Put that down," Sergei said. He took the book away, glanced at it himself and then tucked it in the nearest book-shelf.

"Are we meeting Dr. Afiniganov here?" Vladimir said.

"No. I didn't tell Alexander where we were going."

Young Vlad looked up at Sergei. For a brief moment, Sergei thought he saw a fleeting apprehension in the child's eyes.

"What is it, Vladimir?"

The boy paused.

"It's okay, you can tell me."

"Are you going to sever my phrenic nerve?" Vladimir said.

"No!" Sergei exclaimed. "Of course not. Who told you this?"

"I heard Dr. Afiniganov talking about it with a nurse."

"Do you even know where your phrenic nerve is located?" Sergei said, adjusting his tie.

Slowly the boy looked down at his lap.

Sergei let out a hearty laugh. "Vlad, my boy, that's not your phrenic nerve."

This was not funny to Vladimir. "I don't care. I don't want them to take my phrenic nerve away."

"If you don't know where it is or even what it is — how could you miss it?"

"I just would."

Sergei stopped laughing and leaned in close to where he could feel Vladimir's hiccups against his skin. "Listen to me carefully," he said. "I don't care what Alexander said. I will never allow that to happen. No one is going to cut you up. I promise you that. You aren't just my patient, Vladimir — I think of you as my son. And I take direct responsibility for the fact that your affliction continues to this day. I've made it my life's work to cure you. One day you will sleep through the night without drugs. You will run and play like the other boys and you will grow up to be a strong, important man. In my search for a cure, I've put you through agony. I suppose at the time I thought it was necessary. But I want you to know that if I could, I would switch places with you in an instant. I'm sorry for everything you've been forced to endure. And I swear I'll never let anyone hurt you again."

Sergei looked into Vladimir's mirrorless eyes. There was no reaction to his passionate speech.

Across the room, the door swayed opened, sending a rush of musty air against the bookshelves. A diminutive, troll-like creature emerged from the other side with canes in both hands and giant bushy eyebrows. The light silhouetted him from behind and Vladimir couldn't quite see the creature's face. Its shadowy outline approached.

"Sergei!"

"Markus!" Sergei stood up to embrace the silhouette.

Now Vladimir could see the face of this man. It was more horrible than he could have imagined. Markus had a long, crooked nose centering two crossed eyes, which were small on his face yet impossible to ignore, so wide were his pupils that no discernable trace of white was visible on either side. The hands holding his canes contained an uneven number of fingers; three digits plus a thumb on his left and just an index finger and half a thumb on the right. His hair too was a peculiar sight. Entirely bald on one side, the other side was divided into two sections — thick brown strands in the front and long, shiny gray locks toward the back. Despite Markus's impeccable dress (his shirt was pressed and clean, his tie knotted properly and the right length for his frame), the man smelled faintly of moldy cheese. When he spoke, his words were coated with a drawl-affected accent the likes of which Vladimir had never before heard. This creature's startling visage was an assault to sight, smell and hearing. Not even in the deepest recesses of Vladimir's mind could he imagine what harm this creature might inflict on his other senses.

Sergei held his friend by the shoulders and took a long, admiring look at him, then turned to Vladimir.

"I would like to introduce you to my dear friend Markus."

The dwarfling offered his hand to the boy.

Vladimir refused to shake it.

"Where are your manners?" Sergei said. "Shake the man's hand."

Vladimir reached out and touched the flaccid, malleable skin on Markus's hand. This was not good. Touch had been established. Could taste be that far behind?

"Markus is British," Sergei said.

"He's a capitalist then," Vladimir said.

"In my former life, I suppose I was." Markus breathed directly on the boy. Vladimir recoiled as though the creature was billowing flames from its nose. He took two solid steps back and yelped as he moved. "It seems this boy has a case of the hiccups," Markus said. "Would you like me to get him a glass of water?"

"Oh, my friend," Sergei sighed. "It's much more complicated than that."

"Nonsense," he said. "I know how to solve this quickly and effectively . . . Boo!" Markus screeched. He flared his nostrils and threw his canes in the air.

Young Vladimir stood in place, unfazed. His only reaction was to close his eyes and plug his nose, so wary was he of letting this hirsute gnome's air inside his own body.

Markus scratched the hairy side of his head. "Strange," he said. "That usually does the trick."

Sergei leaned down and whispered a long sentence in his friend's ear. When he finished, the look on Markus's misshapen face was one of astonishment. He leaned forward to examine Vladimir more closely.

"Really?" he said.

Sergei nodded.

"What forms of treatment have you attempted?" Markus said. "Did you try electroshock? What about temporary suffocation?"

"I think," Sergei said, "that it's best we discuss the details of this case in private."

Vladimir was left alone in the stuffy room while the two men engaged in an extended conversation on the other side of the door, their words dampened by the thick wall. Scarcely an audible sound slipped through the crack where the door met its frame, but from what Vladimir could discern, Sergei was asking Markus for help. "I need this from you, old friend," Sergei was saying. Vladimir quickly lost interest and busied himself by retrieving another graphic text from the shelves. Entitled *Attack Patterns of the Female Tiger*, this book contained pictures of a series of human carcasses, each torn apart and partially consumed by the great ravenous cat. While at first only moderately intrigued, as the minutes went by, Vladimir flipped through the pages with eager glee, the sight of each ghastly corpse sending a flush of endorphins rushing to his brain where, in a pang of delight, the opiate receptors swelled to near-euphoric levels. Finally he settled on one picture, that of a man's half-eaten torso entangled in a mesh of barbed wire. Between each convulsive yelp, Vladimir contemplated this man's last desperate moments, how fraught with distress they must have been, how his innate urge for self-preservation must have sent a surge of adrenaline through his body so powerful that had he survived, his life would have been forever changed. Vladimir lifted his small hand and placed it on the page. He closed his eyes and leaned his head back, wondering in his rapidly evolving, child-sized brain which it was better to be — the carnivore or the dying man.

Fifteen minutes later, Sergei and Markus emerged from the other side of the door. Quickly, young Vladimir wiped away the froth from the edges of his mouth. He shut the book as though he'd been caught looking at something scandalous and perverse.

Sergei crouched down to face the boy. "Now, Vladimir, I'm going to leave you with my friend Markus. He just wants to talk to you for a while, to see if there's anything he can do to help your condition. Is that okay?"

Young Vlad watched Markus heave his way through a painful-looking, phlegm-induced cough. He shook his head, stood up from the couch and moved to Sergei's side. Vladimir positioned Sergei as a barrier between him and the creature.

"I promise that Markus won't hurt you," Sergei said. "Don't be afraid."

Vladimir shot Sergei an angry look. "Don't leave me," he said.

"Please," Sergei said, "do this for me."

Vladimir's eyes drifted toward the doorway. Before Sergei knew what was happening, Vladimir turned around and bolted for the door. The boy made it farther than he might have expected; he even grasped the door handle in his small hands before Sergei grabbed him by the waist and tugged him away from the exit. A struggle broke out between the two of them in which the child disobeyed his doctor for the first time. Vladimir kicked and screamed, flailing his arms frantically. Unable to reach anything bolted down, he grabbed an empty Armenian urn from a side table and struck Sergei several times on the head. Sergei, for his part, struggled valiantly to control the child. Markus had taken a step back when the mêlée began and was waiting patiently for it to end.

And end it did. Nearly twenty minutes later, after Sergei had left nursing a budding bruise on his temple and the glass urn lay in ruins on the waiting-room floor, Vladimir was finally alone with Markus in the man's office. The two of them — afflicted child and impurely bred kobold — sat directly across from one another in non-matching leather chairs. Vladimir, suddenly temperamental for the first time since his affliction began, shot Markus a loathsome glare.

"Has Sergei told you what I do for a living?" Markus said.

Vladimir stared straight ahead, hiccupping every 3.7 seconds. He refused to acknowledge his captor.

"I'm a doctor," Markus said. "But not in the way Sergei is a doctor. I'm a practitioner of the mind. A brain scientist, if you will. Sergei thought it might be beneficial for you to talk to me."

"There's nothing wrong with my brain," Vladimir said.

"I'm not suggesting there is," Markus said. "But unless we delve deep into the recesses of your mind and actually see what's in there that makes you tick, we'll never know for sure. I want to know what's going on inside your head, Vladimir. Let's start with something simple. Tell me, what makes you angry? What makes you sad?"

Vladimir didn't answer. When Sergei came back for Vladimir an hour later, the child had still not responded to his interrogator. Markus had tried in vain to elicit a response by asking nearly every probing question in his repertoire, from the straightforward and factual "How old are you?" to the thought-provoking "What do you think your mother is doing right now?" Nothing worked. The child steadfastly refused to speak. This went on for four whole sessions, totaling nearly five hours over the span of a week. Markus would lob question upon question into the air while young Vlad stared back at him with a look of disdain.

"What's your favorite flower?

"Would you rather own a cat or a dog?

"Can a socialist state truly protect the rights of the individual?"

Vladimir struggled with Sergei before each session. He would refuse to get into the vehicle on the way to Markus's office. Once they arrived, he'd refuse to leave the vehicle. After the first two visits, young Vlad stopped making a scene in the waiting room but he would always plead with his eyes for Sergei to stay, and as soon as his doctor returned at the end of the visit, Vladimir would run up and grab hold of his leg, anxious to return to the hospital where Sergei would be forced to administer the numbing drugs that allowed his patient to sleep at night.

In the tenth minute of the fifth session, Markus was busy inventing more questions when suddenly Vladimir's eyes perked. He sat at attention in his chair. "What is it?" Markus said.

Young Vlad seemed unsure whether he should speak.

"Was it something I said?" Markus's excitement grew. "Let me see, what was I going on about? I asked you about trains. Then I asked you about wool socks. No, that's not right. I asked you about cotton socks, layered cotton socks. Was that it?"

Vladimir stared blankly and hiccupped in Markus's direction.

"No, it probably wasn't the socks. Oh, I know. I asked you about love. Have you ever been in love, Vladimir?"

"Yes," the boy said.

Markus leaned back. His uneven teeth formed an optimistic smile. "So, the hiccupping child does speak," he said. "I was beginning to think you would never talk again. Tell me, who did you love?"

"Ileana, a girl in my class."

"And you loved her?"

"Very much."

Markus felt a nervous orange energy in his stomach. He was finally getting through to the boy. "Do you still love her now?"

Vladimir leaned forward, and when he did, his eyes possessed a grave intent far beyond his years. "No," he said.

The orange energy in Markus's stomach, which inspired elation only a physician of the mind can feel the moment a patient displays the initial signs of a breakthrough — and not just manageable therapeutic advancement in this case but rather the very first sign of the apparent and credible mental amelioration of a disquieted, grief-panged soul — transformed instantly into a sickening brown sludge that threatened to expel itself at any moment. Vladimir's tone conveyed such wrath, such piercing intent, that Markus's jovial expression immediately fled and was replaced by pure, unbridled fear.

"Why don't you love her anymore?" Markus said.

"Because . . ." Vladimir started talking. And for the next hour he didn't stop.

"Never again, my friend, never again," Markus said.

Just three minutes before, Sergei had popped his head into Markus's office, an unsuspecting expression on his face. Without hesitation Vladimir hopped off his chair, walked over and stood beside his doctor. Sergei patted the boy on the head and asked Markus if they were still scheduled to meet again at the same time on Monday. Markus, who for the past hour had gripped his canes tighter and tighter until he felt a numbing, wistful ache in his hands, stood up, precariously at first, his canes quivering in wide, haphazard shakes, and fled the room, knocking over a stack of papers on his way out — anything to evade Vladimir's penetrating stare. Sergei stood in place, dumbfounded, the hiccupping boy clinging to his pant leg.

Fifteen minutes later, Sergei was watching Vladimir from the window of Markus's office. He had taken the boy across the street to a café and purchased him a *syrniki* — cheese and apple pancake — as a treat, then left him outside with strict instructions not to speak to anyone. Sergei was wary of allowing Vladimir to roam free after having spent so much time inside the hospital. From the window, young Vlad appeared to be behaving himself. He was kneeling beside Sergei's automobile on a patch of lawn the snow had forgotten, absently pulling frozen strands of grass from the ground with one hand as he devoured the pastry in the other.

Sergei offered his friend a cup of coffee from the café. "Lots of sugar with a few drops of milk?" he said with a forced smile. Markus's tiny misshapen hands reached out with great reluctance and drank down the lukewarm beverage in one swift gulp. Not even the sweet taste of sugar could rid Markus of his dour countenance. Sergei would have to be careful. His old friend had the appearance of a wounded animal ready to attack.

"What happened in here?" he said. "Why the histrionics? Why can't Vladimir just wait in the next room?"

"The boy is mentally unstable," Markus said. "That is what happened. You brought me a patient devoid of human emotion, so callous and vile a soul that when he dies the devil himself will be afraid of him."

"Surely you exaggerate."

Markus burst from his chair, his cheeks flushed red with anger. "I am not exaggerating!"

Sergei spoke as calmly as he could. "Were you able to decipher whether the hiccups are a symptom of some larger mental issue? Is there any chance the boy is faking them?"

"Damn it, Sergei! Forget about the hiccups! Who cares if the boy yelps every four seconds? You can't see the forest for the trees, old chap. The hiccups aren't the problem. The boy is a sociopath. That is the problem."

"What do you mean the boy's a sociopath?"

Markus howled his response. "A madman! A lunatic! An antisocial, deranged beast! Whatever description you want to use, Vladimir meets all the requirements."

"But he's just a boy."

"He is for now, old chap. But mark my words — one day that boy will grow into a man, and when he does, he will bring pain and suffering to all those around him. And you, Sergei, will find yourself mired in this evil creature's depraved quagmire."

"Be reasonable," Sergei said. "I've never seen any evidence of this. The boy doesn't lash out. He's never hurt a nurse or an orderly. There's no overabundance of strangled cats on the hospital grounds. Vladimir has met with dozens of doctors over the past year and a half and none of them have reported anything out of the ordinary. He's docile and accommodating almost to a fault. What on Earth did he say to make you come to this conclusion?"

Markus sat down and leaned back in his chair. Almost instantly his anger fled and was replaced by a glazed, gaping fear. He slumped forward, looking much older than the man Sergei had seen that morning. For ten more minutes, Sergei implored Markus to reveal what Vladimir had said. Markus kept shaking his head. He refused to divulge what transpired while he was alone with the boy. The two doctors exchanged words. Markus, resolute, kept repeating the same cryptic command — "You must distance yourself from that child." Eventually, Sergei gave up trying to squeeze blood from a stone. He made his way to leave. Before he shut the door, Markus stood up from his chair.

"This afternoon, I'm going to purchase a pistol," he said. "And from this day forward, I will carry that pistol with me wherever I go. When I'm awake, I'll keep it in my breast pocket. And when I'm asleep, I will have my finger coiled around the trigger under my pillow."

"Whatever for?" Sergei said.

"Because when Vladimir comes for me, and I believe he will, I won't greet him pleasantly or run away. As Christ is my witness, I'll shoot him dead as he stands."

Sergei stood in the doorway with a look of shock on his face. Words escaped him. The doctor Namestikov could only stare at Markus, who returned his gaze with a determined glare of his own. The two old friends remained locked in perpetuity until finally Sergei relented and closed the door. He stood on the other side for a full minute, unsure what to do. Should he apologize to Markus? Should he storm back in and demand an explanation? Sergei didn't believe either would do any good. Markus had passed judgment on Vladimir, and nothing he said or did would change that. Sergei put his hand up to the office door, held it there, then left the waiting room and walked down the staircase to the outside.

The afternoon sky had started to concede to the purple shadows lurking behind the clouds overhead. Sergei walked under a hazy mist of rain and approached Vladimir as he knelt beside the car. Having long finished the *syrniki*, Vladimir was on his knees searching the clear patch of grass. He stood up when he saw Sergei approaching. Something was between Vladimir's fingers. Sergei looked closer to discover a ladybug. Almost immediately, any doubt Sergei had about his charge's character was put to rest. He saw in front of him what he'd always seen — an innocent nine-year-old boy stricken by an unbearable affliction. Markus must have been out of his mind.

"I've named her Kerkira." Vladimir held the miniature red bug up proudly.

"That's very nice," Sergei said. "Now please get in the vehicle. We're going home."

As Vladimir walked around to the passenger's side, Sergei

spotted a burgundy candy-bar wrapper protruding from the boy's back pocket.

"Where did you get that candy?" Sergei said.

Young Vlad didn't respond.

"Answer me," Sergei said. "Did Markus give it to you? No? Then where did you get it?"

Vladimir hesitated and then pointed across the street to the café where Sergei had purchased his coffee. Inside an old shopkeeper was sweeping the floor.

"Did you pay for the candy?"

Vladimir shook his head.

"You must pay for things," Sergei said. "Don't be angry with me. This is an important lesson every boy must learn. Now please go back and return the candy to the shopkeeper."

The boy's blank expression grew tight on his face, his eyes squinting until their whites formed sharp triangles on either side of his irises. Sergei braced himself for an argument when, unexpectedly, Vladimir handed him the ladybug. The good doctor took the little creature on his finger and watched Vladimir march across the street and enter through the café doors.

Sergei climbed inside the automobile and started the engine. He brought the insect up close to inspect it when, from out of the corner of his eye, he witnessed the most peculiar scene through the window of the café. The shopkeeper was standing against the far wall, his hands clutching the sides of his head. Vladimir's thin shoulders and the back of his small head appeared directly in front of the man. From a distance, it looked as though the shopkeeper was backing away. Sergei watched in stunned silence as his young charge reached out his hand to give back the candy. The shopkeeper waved his hands in short, quick gestures. He wouldn't take it.

His face turned red, the top of his bald head too. They were a good eight meters away, but from inside the running car, Sergei could have sworn he saw in the shopkeeper's expression the same curvature of the mouth, the same unfastened apprehension in his eyes, the indistinguishable acceleration of breath accompanying heart and lung distress that he'd seen in Markus's petrified countenance.

The man appeared terrified of young Vladimir.

A few moments passed before Vladimir exited the café and walked back across the street. He rounded the car and took his seat in the passenger's side. In virtual disbelief, Sergei watched the child shut the car door and look up at him with those expressionless eyes.

"What did you say to that man?" he said.

Vladimir hiccupped. His hollow expression remained unchanged.

"Answer me," Sergei said.

The boy continued to stare.

Sergei didn't know what to do. He couldn't remember a time in his adult life in which he'd been quite so confused.

"Wait here," he said. Sergei left the vehicle running and walked briskly across the road. He pushed open the café door and a bell rang to signal his entrance. The shopkeeper was madly sweeping the floor, back and forth, over and over again on the same spot. He stopped immediately when Sergei appeared.

"My good sir," Sergei said, "what did that boy say to you?"

The man didn't respond. He took two steps backward and shook his head, then scurried behind the counter. When Sergei had purchased coffee here less than thirty minutes earlier, the man had been in good spirits. He even chatted with Sergei about current events and jokingly baited him into banter about the extraordinary success of the local women's ice-hockey team. Now the shopkeeper's face was drenched in sweat, his eyes sodden with the beginnings of an incapacitating fear. Sergei stepped forward and, like a prisoner anticipating lashes from the whip, the man trembled, his arms clasped to his chest.

"What did Vladimir say to you?" Sergei said as gently as he could.

"I will ask you to leave my store," the man said.

"Not until you tell me what the child said."

The shopkeeper's yellow teeth dug into his bottom lip.

"Sir, I must insist," Sergei said.

The man slammed his fist down on the counter. A small teacup and saucer had been sitting in the exact location on the console where his fist landed, a tiny stream of steam curling its way into the cool air. The shopkeeper's fist crashed straight into the teacup. Small shards of the fragmented cup scattered across the counter and spilled over onto the floor.

The man paused. He closed his eyes, gathered his faculties and then opened them again. His voice quavered. "Leave my store. Leave my store and never come back!"

Outside the light rain had picked up. Sergei stood in the burgeoning haze, watching the man from outside the shop. Across the street, Vladimir had crawled into the driver's seat and was leaning against the window. Sergei, who'd been observing this child day and night for well over a year now, noticed something for the first time. For an instant — and only an instant — a wicked gleam formed in young Vlad's eyes. Sergei saw in Vladimir what Markus had described. He saw not a child but a creature, an evil spirit bathed in malice. In the distance, a crackle of thunder sounded. The rain began to pour. It coated the streets and turned the snow on the ground into sopping-wet piles of slush. The storm enveloped Sergei and his gaping disbelief. He could deny it no longer.

Vladimir, his prized patient and a child not yet ten years of age, was a monster.

six

Sergei spent much of that evening sitting quietly in his study, deep in thought. He brought his grandfather's pipe out from its casing, dabbed some tobacco in the bowl and lit the pipe for the first time since medical school. There he sat, alone in the dim candlelight, smoking and brooding for hours. Eventually he decided he'd lingered long enough and turned in for the evening at the early hour of 8 p.m.

He knew he'd have trouble falling asleep. Ever since his divorce, Sergei found the process of drifting into unconsciousness a most frustrating experience. Lying quiet and alone in a dark room was an open invitation for sadness and rage to meander into his mind. For a fortnight now, when he placed his head on his soft satin pillow, his ears would ring with the slight laugh his ex-wife had emitted when she saw the slacks he purchased on discount from Slavov's Men's Emporium. Over and over again the laugh transformed from girlish and inadvertent to condescending and deliberate. With her cackle drilling a hole in his soul, to the front of his mind soared the evening under moonlight when she refused his embrace. He remembered the indifference in her touch, how she'd moved to avoid his hand against her back. Each night Sergei would eventually grow so frustrated — with his ex-wife, Asenka, and what she'd done to him, but more with himself for not having the fortitude to move past the aching hurt of her abandonment — that he would stand up in a huff and pace his study,

knock over random objects in sudden stabs of fury and remi-
nisce about his childhood, a time when sleep flowed like a
river, the dreams liquid, the slumber a cage of ecstasis from
which he dared not escape.

This evening was different. Sergei couldn't sleep, but it
had little to do with Asenka. Lying awake, he stared at the
ceiling, careful not to touch his ex-wife's side of the bed, his
thoughts occupied by Vladimir, the hiccups and what horren-
dous thoughts he could only imagine were running through
his patient's troubled mind. He tossed and turned for an
hour before giving up. Briskly, Sergei climbed out of bed and
walked into his study. He picked up the telephone and called
Alexander. An older woman's voice answered.

"Hello?"

"Is Alexander there?"

"I'm sorry but the doctor is out for the evening. Would
you like to leave a message?"

"Who is this?" Sergei said.

"I'm the maid. Doctor Afiniganov is out for the evening."

"Yes, I know. You already said that," Sergei said. "Where
is he?"

There was silence on the other end.

"I'm one of his colleagues from the hospital," Sergei said.
"It is imperative that I get in contact with Alexander immediately."

"Is this an emergency, sir?" she said.

"Yes, of course it is. Do you think I would call for any
other reason?"

She paused. "No."

"Do you take me for an idiot?"

"Of course not."

Sergei's voice raised. "I am an important man. I have

performed open heart surgery and devised treatments that abated a plague of leprosy," he said, unable to contain himself. "My professional opinion is held in such high regard that heads of state come to me personally to perform their physicals. I even finished at the top of my class at Imperial Tomsk University's medical school." His voice built to a crescendo as he stated the year, month and day of his graduation.

"Didn't Doctor Afiniganov finish first in the class at Tomsk that year?" the woman said. "I was working for his father at that time and, if I correctly recall, Alexander finished with the highest accolades ever bestowed upon a graduate of the school . . ."

"Nonetheless, I assure you . . ."

". . . there was even a ceremony in which he was given a plaque with his name and 'First in Class' on it. The plaque is on the wall in the doctor's study . . ."

"Listen to me . . ."

". . . I can get it for you if you like. It's beautiful. And made of real gold."

"I don't care about the damned plaque!" Sergei said. "Just tell me where Alexander is."

"He's attending a formal function at the Isirk Ballroom. It's a black-tie affair . . ."

"Thank you." Sergei slammed the phone down. In a fury, he knocked over a Romanian *blajini* carving, a prized heirloom from his mother's side, and then fell to the floor. He held his head in his hands and curled up in the fetal position against the far wall. Sergei fought back tears. To the outside world, he was a powerful, successful man. The mothers of his patients swooned when he entered the room. The state paid him well. His life was filled with extravagance. He lived in an enormous house with two servants in a splendid neighborhood and could have any woman he desired. But his entire life, he'd lived in Alexander's shadow. Were it not for Alexander, that gold plaque would be on Sergei's wall. His divorce from Asenka had stripped him of his confidence and now he found himself a grown man, unable to cure a simple case of the hiccups, cradled in a ball on the floor wearing pajamas with a rip in the rear end while his rival dined with dignitaries at a ballroom to which Sergei had never been invited.

Enough of this.

Sergei rose to his feet and marched down the hall to his bedroom. He tore off his pajamas, wiped his armpits with a wet rag and pulled his best blue suit from the closet. Sergei stood in front of the full-length mirror, completely naked, his pajamas in one hand, his suit in the other. "Tatiana!" he cried at the top of his lungs. "Tatiana! Come here!"

From two flights down, Sergei's maid heard his cries and came running. A homely creature with modest breasts and a large backside, Tatiana had long awaited this call. At the exact moment Sergei called out her name, she had been in the kitchen, drawing an inverted heart on a pad of paper, dreaming of Sergei and how she wished he would come to her at night and take her against the cold washbasin in her room. She'd long imagined what it would feel like to have her face forced against the frigid steel while he ravaged her from behind. Oh, the rapture of it all! She bounded up the stairs with delight, each step taking her closer to the man she'd loved from afar so very long. Her loins, warm and aching from years of solitude, yearned for Sergei as she reached the top floor. "Yes, Doctor?" She opened the door to her master's bedroom. "Aieeee!"

Tatiana shrieked out loud. She hadn't expected Sergei's naked body to be standing in front of her, holding a suit in one hand, his other hand plying open the hole in the buttocks of a pair of pajamas. *No, no, no, no!* she screamed in her mind. This wasn't how it was supposed to be. *Sergei should be wearing a smoking jacket with a sash across his waist.*

"Dear God, child." Sergei stepped back. Quickly he shielded his genitals with his suit.

"I'm sorry, sir," Tatiana said and covered her eyes.

"Our protocol is to speak through the door."

"Again, I'm sorry," she said.

"Call Afin and have him start the car."

"Yes, Doctor."

"And please knock next time."

"Yes, Doctor."

"And if you would have these sewn for me . . ." He tossed his pajamas in the direction of the mortified girl.

Tatiana caught the pajamas on her head, begged forgiveness, then sped a hasty retreat from the room. Alone again in his bedroom and completely nude, Sergei smiled in the corner of his mouth. He put on his suit and fashioned himself in front of the mirror. Tonight would have an upward turn after all.

Sergei — doctor, divorcer and man-about-town — was going out for the evening.

Sergei stepped out of his vehicle and straight into a muddy puddle of slush. His driver, Afin, an elderly Polish man with fading eyesight, a cheerful disposition and the profile of a swollen warthog, had failed him again by parking too far from the curb. At the last function Sergei attended, his driver had made a scene when he referred to the ambassador's daughter as a "treat for the eyes." Two functions before that, Afin had inadvertently driven home the wrong couple, infuriating Sergei's then-wife and launching her into a hysterical tirade aimed not only at Sergei's virility but also at the ethnicity of their hosts that evening. It had taken Sergei an hour to calm his wife down, just enough time for Afin to return and pile them into the car alongside the couple he'd mistakenly driven.

This Afin was a curious sort. Clumsy, absent-minded and often confused, the man had revealed nothing to Sergei about his past. Five years earlier, Sergei hired Afin on the recommendation of an acquaintance without troubling to ask for further references or even insisting the old man have his vision tested. Sergei felt vaguely sorry for him. In his more befuddled moments, Afin would stumble about like a silent-movie star, unintentionally exaggerating his movements, his arms gesticulating wildly as he struggled to regain his footing after slipping on the wet stone driveway. Sergei wasn't aware of his driver's more contemplative moments, when Afin would sit alone in a dark and quiet room — disconnected from his affable civility and bumbling demeanor — and struggle to come to terms with the life he had led.

Years ago while working for the state, Afin had put 249 men to their death. Some were hanged. Others were beheaded. Occasionally, the two went hand in hand as the head of a hanged man popped right off his body and landed with a bloody thud at Afin's feet. Now long retired, Afin routinely fluctuated his perspective on his role in the executions. Some days he would bury his face in his hands, mystified as to how a sweet little Polish boy could have grown into a monster. Other days he wouldn't give the 249 souls a second thought. It was only a job. The state killed those men, after all. His hands were simply the instruments of their concentrated minds. Afin never intended any malice. He was much happier now, he decided, driving Sergei back and forth from work and occasionally straining his murky vision to give Tatiana a wayward glance.

"I'm sorry, sir," Afin said as he helped Sergei step over the slush.

"Not to worry." Sergei shook the water from his best pair of shoes. "Wait here, please. I'll be right out." Sergei walked up to the grand entrance of the Isirk Ballroom. A national treasure that through sheer luck and good fortune had escaped the destruction of the Bolshevik War, its looming arches, high ceilings and majestic artwork made the ballroom the central meeting place for Moscow's most affluent citizens. Sergei ignored the splendor and stormed straight through the front doors on a mission to find Alexander. He was stopped at the ice sculpture in the main lobby by a maître d' and two doormen.

"May I see your invitation?" the maître d' said in a thick French accent.

"I have no invitation," Sergei said. "I've come to see one of my colleagues from the hospital."

"Are you a doctor?"

"Yes." Sergei fished his medical license out from his jacket and showed it to the man.

"Is this an emergency?"

"Yes, it is."

"Is someone going to die?"

"Well, no."

"Is someone in imminent danger?"

"Imminent? No," Sergei said.

"Then I'm afraid I can't permit you inside," the man said.

Sergei peered over the shoulders of the guards. Inside he could see Moscow's elite hobnobbing about in front of the lavish buffet in the great hall. He couldn't quite make out who was who, his view partially obscured by the protruding fin of a sea nymph cut into the ice.

"I must get inside." Sergei stepped past the man. Immediately, the two guards blocked his way. "You don't understand —" he gasped, his sentence cut off when one of the guards thumped him hard on the chest.

"No," the maître d' said. "It is you who does not understand. Invitations were sent out for this event six months ago. Each of the guests attending has made a considerable donation in support of our new indoor garden. We can't let in just anyone off the street, let alone a man in a blue suit."

Sergei looked down at his suit and then up at the three men standing in front of him. Each was wearing a black tuxedo, their white shirts adorned with a black bow tie. He looked back at his suit, with his right leg soaked up to the knee, and wondered what others secretly must think when they see him walking down the street.

"This is my finest attire," Sergei said.

The maître d' fashioned an uppity sneer.

Sergei turned to walk away. "Fine, if you're willing to take the risk."

"What risk?" the maître d' said.

Sergei stopped at the doors. "The risk of all your patrons growing violently ill. There is a man in there, a colleague of mine from the hospital who came into contact with a very sick patient today. The patient's symptoms include painful vomiting, spontaneous dysentery and an unexplained excretion of mucus from not one, not two, but three orifices. It's almost certain that my colleague is contagious and I've come here to save these people from what could very well be the most painful, embarrassing night of their lives."

"You're lying," the maître d' said.

"Believe what you want to believe." Sergei started to walk away. "Do not blame me when your patrons become sick all over your ballroom floor."

He was halfway out the front doors when the maître d' came up behind him and petitioned Sergei to find the contagious man. The doctor Namestikov, his lies accepted as fact, felt a great satisfaction until the maître d' insisted he change from his blue suit jacket into a more formal black jacket.

"No," Sergei said. "People will assume that I couldn't find a matching pair of pants. These colors look ridiculous next to one another. I'll be a laughing stock in a mismatched suit."

"Nonsense," the maître d' said. He helped Sergei off with his coat and into the formal black jacket. "You won't be inside but for a moment anyways. If I were to allow you to wear blue, you would draw even more attention to yourself."

Sergei insisted again but the man was adamant. The only way Sergei would be allowed into the great hall was if he was wearing a black jacket. With extreme reluctance, Sergei slipped the jacket over his shoulders. Its sleeves carried with them the pliant odor of whiskey and Croatian perfume. Sergei pressed out the wrinkles against his chest and allowed the larger of the two guards to brush the dust off his shoulders, then he stepped past the ice sculpture and into the great hall. It was difficult for him to maintain an air of dignity, what with the mismatched clothes, the soaking-wet loafer and the undeniable suspicion that he'd forgotten to properly trim his ears of all errant hairs, but Sergei soldiered on past the women in evening gowns dipping cake into the cheese fondue and the politicians congratulating one another as they smoked cigars. He made his way past the extensive buffet table without giving a thought to pinching a snack when he stopped at the last tray of desserts.

Before Sergei lay an extravagant safari scene with lions carved out of truffles and peacock-shaped pineapples. Everywhere Sergei looked a new treasure was to be found, from apricot trees to candy-stick villagers drowning in the chocolate mousse quicksand. The very sight of this sticky-sweet smorgasbord was overwhelming. Sergei's eyesight, never an issue during his adult years, started to fail him the longer he stared at the dazzling whites and bright oranges. The air wavered as though it were hot inside; the skeletonized shapes of the sugars crystallized into an onslaught of garish glittering opulence and at the same time grew murky, fragmented. Suddenly the table vanished, a mass of refracted light mobilized in its place. Sergei felt dizzy. A painful swell developed in his chest as an epidemic of panic threatened to overtake him. Sergei hunched forward and placed his hands on the table, his thumb dipped into a pool of blue gelatin. Oh, how he longed for the warm, insomnious comfort of his bed. Why had he ever left home? What purpose could it serve to accost his rival here in this place where he so clearly did not belong?

With a shudder, Sergei turned to leave and was met face-to-face by Alexander in all his black-tuxedo glory. As though a chandelier had fallen from the ceiling, Sergei's eyesight returned in a sudden crash. Alexander gasped in surprise. The two men stared at one another in staggering astonishment, taking turns opening their mouths with nothing emerging, the air between them forming a vacuous stupor before finally Alexander spoke.

"Your jacket doesn't match your pants."

Sergei lowered his eyes in a descending arc toward his torso, his gaze focusing on each fuzzy piece of lint and microbe of bacteria left behind by the innumerable souls who, trapped by destiny or desperation, had been forced against their wills into the confines of this black prison. Sergei wanted to turn around right now and bolt from the ballroom. Only his body refused. His legs took root in the ground, his arms constrained as those of a lunatic wrapped up in an asylum. Sergei paused and stammered. He briefly considered an honorable suicide through some sort of staged accident involving perhaps an attack by an outraged animal or a tragic yet credible fall from a great height, before feeling within himself a surge of adrenaline. Deep from the kidney gland it mobilized, the first gush invigorating, the second and third sending stabbing swells to his brain. At that very moment in front of the dessert tray, he found in himself a strength he had never known. He would stand up to this torment. Out of all the moments in his life, this would be the one he would finally seize. No longer would he be forced to live under the crushing weight of Alexander's shadow. No longer would he endure a sleepless night as his nemesis's voice careened about his head. Sergei mobilized his courage, composed himself and then spoke plainly and clearly.

"The coordination of my ensemble is none of your concern. I have sought you out tonight on a matter of great importance, of our young patient Vladimir . . ."

"Yes, yes, the hiccups. That is fine," Alexander said. He seemed uncharacteristically anxious. His eyes shifted around the room.

"No, old friend, it is not fine. Our patient has hidden from us a depravity of mind, not a lunacy as I suspected, but a villainous immorality verging on pure, unbridled evil."

"Evil, you say?"

"Something sinister and vile resides in his soul. He's hidden it from us all along. In all my years, I've never seen anything like it . . ."

Alexander placed his hand on the small of Sergei's back. "We can discuss Vladimir's case at the hospital on Monday. You should leave now."

"No!" Sergei pulled away. "You will not send me home. I will be heard."

From nearby, partygoers turned toward Sergei's raised voice, their faces ranging from curiosity in the far corners to disapproval closer to the buffet, culminating in the outright condemnation on the face of a woman Sergei had accidentally bumped into, forcing her sausagey fingers to impale the lemon tart she'd been in the process of selecting. From the foyer, the maître d' and his two doormen came marching through the crowd. Sergei had very little time.

"I beg of you," Alexander said, "you must leave. You were not invited."

Alexander's entire countenance had an air of suspicion about it. Sergei had never seen him so nervous. During his day-to-day activities at the hospital, in his dealings with patients, even the difficult ones with the troublesomely incurable afflictions, Alexander always maintained a firm air of formality, never joking, at all times securing his emotions behind a reserved wall of poise and self-assurance. In his hasty attempt to usher Sergei from the ballroom, Alexander's pupils had dilated. His brow glossed with the first showings of perspiration. Alexander's hands shook — the very hands that that afternoon had reached inside the open chest cavity of a patient and with delicate precision massaged the patient's atrioventricular valve, saving the patient from a major hemorrhage and almost certain death. These hands, the steadiest in all the republic, were trembling in Sergei's black and blue presence.

At last, Sergei thought, *I have the best of him.*

"What's the matter?" Sergei said. "Has the physician finally been failed by his steady hand?"

Before his rival could respond, a familiar aroma rose in volumes to the embattled doctor's nose. So faint that no one save Sergei could discern it from the buffet's miscellaneous odors, it flowed to him like a wave, this enchanting elixir created by the merging of a sumptuous lilac perfume with a natural skin scent so intoxicating it could have come from only one woman — Asenka. Sergei's ex-wife approached the two men from behind. The doctor Namestikov forgot all about Alexander and turned to see Asenka's ageless beauty, her wide shimmering blue eyes. Sergei's heart skipped a beat. He remembered instantly why he'd fallen in love with her. All of the moments he'd spent agonizing and blaming himself — smashing heirlooms in his office late at night and curling up in tears on his bathroom floor — were instantly forgotten. She was within a meter of him now. Oh, how Sergei wished she would run up and embrace him. All would be forgiven.

But she did not embrace him. Asenka sauntered straight into the waiting arms of his rival. At this moment, exactly seven months, one day, nine hours and four minutes since Sergei had begun working with Alexander, his ex-wife placed a kiss flush on Alexander's lips.

"Hasn't Alexander told you?" she said. "We're in love."

Astonished, Sergei's brain slowed to a Neanderthal crawl. His synapses fired with lethargy. It was as if Sergei's body were somehow striving to keep his soul from grasping how truly belittling this moment was. The desperate look he'd initially given Asenka now reeked of weakness. How crudely obvious he had been, displaying his dopey-eyed pleadings before the entire room. Sergei looked from Alexander to Asenka and back to Alexander again. His rival's face flushed with embarrassment. Alexander even appeared contrite. In the recesses of his mind, Sergei thought perhaps somehow he could one day understand Alexander's role in all of this. But he could never forgive Asenka for what she'd done — for what she was doing even now at this very moment. Just the sight of her, with her full-length white gown accentuating the magnificence of her every curve, her long gloves and dark smoking pen, those wondrous bright blue eyes — everything about her enraged Sergei. He hated her magnificent cheekbones and chiseled pert little nose. He hated her very existence.

Sergei's gaze drifted to Asenka's purse where, from out of the far corner, popped the head of the smallest dog ever bred in Russia. The blue Chihuahua, named for the subtle hint of indigo in its coat, had been banned by the government. At issue was the inbreeding process that produced a high number of deformities. To get that blue Chihuahua, the average litter of five dogs included at minimum four with unspeakably gross birth defects. This was the prize animal to escape the womb intact, the only one out of a hundred deemed fit for sale. It was a marvel of science that this little creature had survived. And all Sergei wanted to do was strangle it with his bare hands.

"Old friend . . ." Alexander said.

"Do not speak," Sergei said.

Asenka let out a caustic laugh. "Sergei," she said, "your jacket doesn't match your pants."

A tempest formed within Sergei. His rage, simmering now for months, finally reached full boil. Asenka had kissed his enemy right in front of him! And he had accepted her embrace. Still she languished in his arms! Now she dared to take issue with what he was wearing? What he had been forced to wear? Good Lord, was there no limit to the injustice?

In a sudden spastic motion, Sergei ripped the black jacket off his body and threw it wildly to the ground. His eyes glazed over. He clenched his fists and stepped forward.

"Be reasonable," Alexander said.

But Sergei was beyond all reason. He reached out and grabbed Alexander by the collar. Before he could throttle him, the two doormen took hold of Sergei and a small skirmish erupted. The doormen wrestled Sergei to the ground only to find they were unable to hold him there; so great was Sergei's fury that he struggled to his feet and made another unsuccessful lunge at Alexander. Asenka stepped forward and slapped Sergei square across the face, leaving a red mark that would last for days. Sergei, however, would not be deterred. He stumbled back against the buffet table, surrounded on all sides by the angry doormen, a befuddled Alexander and his malicious concubine. In the midst of it all, the maître d' was bellowing out orders to anyone who would listen.

Sergei was about to be overcome. In a moment of panic, he reached back and grasped the large punch bowl, still three quarters full of bright red juice and an assortment of fruit slices. He lifted it above his head and threatened the growing crowd.

"Stand back," he said. "I will splash you all."

"Think of what you're about to do," the maître d' said.

"Yes, Sergei. Put it down," Alexander said.

From the back, dozens of voices joined in.

"Don't throw it."

"You'll ruin my dress."

"For the love of God, man, you're at a formal function!"

Each of them pleaded with Sergei to set the bowl down. Every voice, that is, except Asenka's. She stepped to the front of the crowd and faced Sergei eye to eye.

"Do not fear, good people." She raised her arms with

authority. "Sergei will not throw the bowl. It's just not in his nature. He doesn't have the nerve to do it."

Sergei stared straight at Asenka, who in turn looked back at him fearlessly. She was surrounded by a thicket of Moscow's elite, nearly two hundred of them now, all in formal attire, all out for an evening when Sergei had been expected to remain home in his bed, stewing about those who'd done him wrong. In his heart, he questioned whether he truly had the gumption to thrust the fruit punch on them. He'd lived his whole life strictly abiding by society's rules. That hadn't changed yet. Were he to set the bowl down, he still might be able to use his considerable charm to make light of the situation, to elicit a laugh from the swarming mass and perhaps even ingratiate himself with his hosts. It wasn't too late to turn back. Sergei could exit of his own accord. He could leave Alexander and Asenka to canoodle together in front of these bastards and he would be none the worse off. Yes, Sergei could have left with his dignity intact.

But what good is dignity when it is coated in regret?

In one fluid motion, Sergei raised the bowl to the rafters and dumped its entire contents over Asenka's pure white gown. He conked her over the head with the bowl for good measure. She screamed a bloody scream and then collapsed. Her dress turned red, pink and orange in splotches. Ice cubes tumbled into her bosom. Sergei stood above her triumphantly, his hands raised in a V, a jubilant smile stretched from ear to ear.

One second passed and then two. Then Sergei was tackled, his face planted into the ground. A mêlée ensued in which Sergei — kicking, screaming and even biting — was dragged out of the Isirk Ballroom.

★ ✳ ★

Alexander stood over an ailing Asenka. He thought not about her welfare, nor the ultimate disgrace of his rival. Beside him, tracked across the marble floor, were the birdlike paw prints of the world's smallest dog. Alexander knew he would be charged with retrieving the animal from whatever fat lady's gown it had sought sanctuary under. Only he couldn't manage to organize his thoughts well enough to begin the search. Inevitably, he kept returning to the same thought over and over again. It loitered in his mind, slowly pressing against the forefront of his skull.

Vladimir. The boy with the tragic case of the hiccups. Sergei had said the child wasn't insane. It was something much worse. What could it be? What was it, Alexander wondered, that made Sergei storm in here like a madman? What was this evil that lurked beneath the surface of the young boy?

seven

Alexander Afiniganov had long been a man of action. Alternately stern and callous, he had a reputation for lapses into ill-temperament. Quick was his rise to ire when he had the occasion to contend with fools and slow was his patience when confronted by those not matching his superior intellect. Unlike Sergei, Alexander wasn't tortured by personal demons. From the moment he lay his head on his pillow at night until the moment he woke in the morning, he slept the peaceful sleep of a man content with his role in this world. To those who hardly knew him, Alexander was an acerbic character, obsessed with his own brilliance and incapable of regard for the feelings of others. To those who knew him well, he was not only short-tempered and inconsiderate but also conceited and utterly humorless.

Above all things, Alexander was self-aware. He knew others were afraid to socialize with him in the hospital cafeteria and reluctant to seek his professional advice for fear of being disparaged were they even slightly mistaken in their diagnosis. Rather than dissuade his peers of this notion, Alexander did everything in his power to encourage his reputation as a difficult, gifted intellectual. In his heart he knew that when stripped of all the social baggage and cleansed of his brusque demeanor, Alexander Afiniganov was a compassionate man who did what needed to be done.

No more obvious was his empathy than when his rival was

dragged by his heels out of the Isirk Ballroom. Alexander felt for Sergei Namestikov in spite of everything Sergei had put him through. Ever since grade school, Sergei had been a thorn in Alexander's side, always competing with him and keeping every manner of tally in an imaginary contest of which Alexander wanted no part. Alexander understood why he did it. Sergei needed an antagonist whose success he could use as a benchmark for his own accomplishments. It was this adversarial relationship that drove Sergei to great heights both academically and professionally. Alexander, on the other hand, needed no external motivation and considered his rivalry with Sergei to exist mostly in Sergei's own head. When he finished first in his class at Tomsk, he did so based on an inherent desire to push his intellectual capacity to new levels. He didn't care that Sergei finished second (a distant second, Alexander might add). When his award-winning paper on phobias was published, Alexander dismissed Sergei's moaning over the timing of its release. He wrote that paper for a personal sense of pride, not the satisfaction of besting someone else. Even when he bedded Asenka, it wasn't to hurt Sergei. Alexander did so because fornicating with a beautiful, alluring woman was what a great man would do.

Now, despite his sympathy for Sergei, Alexander had to do what was right in the case of young Vladimir. Though loath to admit it, Alexander had never been so mystified by an illness as he was by Vladimir's incurable hiccups. Initially, he applied thoughtful analysis and deliberate consideration in his quest to find their root cause. Then days turned into weeks and weeks turned into months. For the first time in his career, Alexander began grasping at straws. He unintentionally allowed a randomness to enter into his ever-changing assessment of the boy's condition. Poor Vladimir was made to endure uncomfortable, often excruciating examinations, all in the hope they might inadvertently stumble upon a cure.

One afternoon while sitting down on the toilet to rid himself of a bothersome batch of *zharkoye*, Alexander had an epiphany. Vladimir's case was untreatable through modern medical procedures. In fact, the hiccups were not the primary point of contention in this patient. Something was wrong deep within the child — not in his body, but in his soul. There was nothing he or Sergei could do. Shortly thereafter, Alexander approached Sergei on the cobblestone path and made his best effort to explain his sudden realization. He remembered a disinterested Sergei staring absently at the snow. Sergei wouldn't listen to him no matter what he said. Incensed by his colleague's demeanor, Alexander worked behind Sergei's back and set a plan in motion. Vladimir would be cured if it was the last thing Alexander did.

Nearly nine days after Sergei's fall from grace, Alexander's plan led him to be sitting in a horse-drawn carriage, traveling up a bumpy dirt road on the side of a mountain in Northern Mongolia with Vladimir asleep in the coach beside him. Across from Alexander was a nurse's aide and riding beside their driver in the icy air atop the carriage was Tarkov, an orderly Alexander had selected specifically for his oxen-like strength and dull wit. Were they to encounter any trouble that Alexander could not talk or buy his way out of, Tarkov would be relied upon to give their assailants a stern thrashing. A month earlier, when the initial arrangements of his plan were put into place, the strapping Siberian was the first piece in Alexander's puzzle. Not only was Tarkov brave and strong, he was also foolhardy enough to demand no more than a single extra day's wage as payment for the dangerous journey. Yes, cheap and stupid — that is how Alexander liked his henchmen.

The nurse's aide, on the other hand, had proved to be quite a more difficult bargain. When Alexander left the Isirk Ballroom, he was so concerned about what Sergei might do with young Vladimir that he moved his plan forward by two weeks. It wasn't good enough to wait until the morning. He had to act immediately. Alexander assisted Asenka home, placed her in bed and then took a car to the hospital and telephoned Tarkov. He woke the muscular oaf from his sleep and demanded Tarkov meet him at the hospital immediately, then set about finding a nurse. At 11 p.m. on a Friday evening it would be difficult to find a nurse willing to accompany them on their journey, let alone one who could maintain a clandestine air about her assignment. Alexander demanded complete secrecy. He would not have Sergei discovering what he'd done and beginning an ill-advised pilgrimage to find the boy. Alexander stormed about the hospital, moving from room to room until he eventually discovered Ilvana Strekov asleep on a chair outside the critical care unit.

"Are you a nurse?" he said.

Ilvana sat up in a fright, startled by the bellowing voice of a senior hospital official.

"No," she said.

"What is your profession?"

"I'm a nurse's aide," she said in her timid voice.

"Good enough." Alexander cleared his throat. "The hospital requires that you accompany me on a trip to a faraway land. The trip should take no more than a few weeks' time and we must leave immediately. It is a matter of some secrecy."

"Why is it a secret?"

"If I told you, my dear, then it wouldn't be a secret."

"And you'll pay me for my time?"

"Yes. But we must leave right away."

Ilvana Strekov scrunched her nose. "I will require more than my regular pay," she said.

Alexander gave her a surprised look. He hadn't expected anything other than complete obedience. This woman must have known he was disregarding hospital procedures and was taking advantage of the situation. She was completely unscrupulous. Alexander respected her already.

"Name your price," he said. "Time is of the essence and I have none to spend bartering with you. What will it be? Rubles? A promotion?"

"I want to be your assistant."

"On the trip?"

"No, here at the hospital," she said.

"That's out of the question. You wouldn't like me. I'm ill-tempered and demanding. Moreover, I already have an assistant."

"Then she can travel with you." Ilvana sat back in her chair.

An image of Alexander's current assistant floated about his brain. A thick-wristed, middle-aged woman of Latvian descent, she was the only assistant who could tolerate his petulant demeanor. The Latvian woman was a perfect aide — competent, intelligent, never tardy and wise enough to know when to leave Alexander alone. This Ilvana Strekov had none of these qualities. Alexander could tell just by looking at her. She was lethargic and had the voice of a retarded child. He would be forced to fire her in a week's time.

"Fine," he said. "Henceforth, you are my assistant. Now quickly, we must go."

Ilvana stood up and followed the doctor. Together with Tarkov, they set about stealing the boy away in the middle of the night.

It took less than an hour for Alexander to regret recruiting Ilvana for their journey. She fell asleep twice before they left the hospital, once in a chair at the side of Vladimir's bed and a second time while standing on her feet waiting for Tarkov to pull around in his automobile. The muscular orderly drove the group to the Yaroslavsky Rail Terminal, where they boarded a train traveling east on the Trans-Siberian line. Ilvana, taxed with the responsibility of keeping Vladimir sedated, proved unpredictable during their four days on the train. She was quite competent during her waking hours. She checked Vladimir's heart rate, monitored his temperature and administered the exact amount of drugs to keep the boy in a hazy, semiconscious state. The problem was keeping Ilvana awake. She fell asleep at the most inopportune times — in the middle of meals, while stepping off the train and often in mid-sentence. During a stop in Tyumen, when they entered a delicatessen to purchase food and water, to Alexander's astonishment the woman pocketed a glass figurine from a shelf near the back of the store and snuck outside with the item, an exhilarated expression on her face. Alexander had half a mind to throw her from the moving railroad car and leave her stranded on the outskirts of Mongolia. He would have too, if he hadn't been so focused on getting Vladimir to their destination.

The boy came to his senses only once while en route through the Circum-Baikal tunnel west of Kultuk. Other than that, he remained sedated all the way to their destination stop at the Siberian city of Irkutsk. There, Alexander met a contact who, for a fee, granted them passage over the Mongolian border without the requisite state-issued documentation. This step eliminated days from their journey, as it normally would have been exceedingly difficult to leave the country with an unconscious, hiccupping child who had no papers.

Once they entered Mongolia, the group boarded a boat and sailed to the south side of the Egiyn River where they were met by a horse-drawn carriage. Its driver — a short, grim, deceitful man with a long mustache and enormous fur coat — was of course crooked. Even though Alexander had paid for his services in advance, the driver demanded an extra fifty percent for the inconvenience of moving the schedule forward two weeks. Alexander had planned for just such a contingency and paid the man without complaint. When they arrived at the base of the Burkhan Khaldun mountain, the driver stopped the horses and demanded additional compensation lest he leave them stranded a hundred kilometers from civilization. Alexander lost his temper and engaged the man in a ferocious argument in broken Khalkha, with sprinklings of Russian and Buryat interspersed throughout. Finally, after uttering disparaging remarks about the man's ancestors and threatening to have Tarkov strangle him, Alexander relented. With only a rough hand-drawn map of their destination, he needed this man not only to steer the carriage along the treacherous mountainside, but also to act as a guide. He handed over more money, climbed back inside, and they were on their way up the mountain. Before reaching the summit, the carriage took a fork in the road and began traveling down toward a valley on the other side.

About twenty minutes before they reached the valley, Vladimir awoke. He had been lying with his head in Ilvana's lap for the last three hours and had been jostled from his sleep when the carriage rumbled through a patch of potholes. Nurse's aide Strekov was too busy resting her eyes to notice. Vladimir's morphine-induced torpor, languid and dense from start to finish, was difficult to emerge from. He sat up, startled but dozy, his eyes wide.

"Relax, child," Alexander said. "I assure you — you're quite safe."

"Where am I?" Vladimir said between hiccups.

"You're in Northern Mongolia. We're on our way down the great Burkhan Khaldun mountain, heading toward the valley on the other side."

Vladimir pointed at the sleeping nurse's aide. He'd left behind a messy puddle of drool in her lap. "Who's she?"

"Her name is Ilvana. You needn't worry. She's harmless. The poor dear sleeps most of the time."

"Where's Doctor Namestikov?"

"I didn't tell Sergei about our journey."

Vladimir's mouth tightened. His penetrating eyes shifted. "Doctor Namestikov is going to be angry," he said.

Up until now, Alexander had given his rival consideration only in abstract terms. For the first time he pictured Sergei storming through the hospital in a frenzy, desperate to find his prized patient. The idea that at this very moment Sergei could be scouring the streets of Moscow, his enraged eyes red as the lining of an admiral's coat, brought a smile to Alexander's face.

"Sergei has done all he can. You're in my care now."

Vladimir cast a glance at the woman and then back at Alexander. He climbed up on his knees and looked out the window into the sea of lush, green foliage and then sat back down and gave Alexander his ever-present vacuous glare.

"Aren't you going to ask me where we're going?" Alexander said.

"I already know where you're taking me."

Alexander leaned forward, his interest piqued. "And where's that?"

"You're taking me to sever my phrenic nerve."

"What would give you that idea?" Alexander said.

"I heard you talking about it with a nurse when you thought I was sleeping."

Alexander responded in perhaps the most gentle tone he'd affected in his entire life. "That was merely one suggestion out of many. We discarded that initiative months ago. You must understand, I'm not trying to cure your hiccups. Suppose I did sever your nerve and by some good fortune you lived through the procedure and were miraculously cured. Would everything be right in your world? Would you be able to go out into society and function like a normal person? Would you grow up into a teenager and then as a man, find employment and start a family?"

Vladimir gave him an empty look.

Alexander continued. "I think there is a deeper problem here. You're a very troubled young boy, Vladimir. I want nothing more than to cure your hiccups. And hopefully someday I'll be able to do that. But first you must quell the crisis in your soul. I'm not sure what's wrong with you. I cannot pinpoint your dilemma and I would be ill-advised to try. It's something you must find within yourself."

Vladimir's expression, for so long a blank page, suddenly morphed into an implacable scowl. "Why do you want to help me?" he said.

Alexander, unprepared for the boy's question, was at a loss for words. "It's my job to help you," he said.

"That's not the only reason. You wouldn't travel to some faraway land just to help one of your patients."

"Nonsense," Alexander said. "I would do this for any of my charges."

"No," Vladimir said. "It's something else. You're afraid of something. What is it that you're afraid of?"

Alexander was slowly growing more and more

uncomfortable in the presence of this child. For the first time during their journey, he wished Ilvana would wake from her stupor. "It's not that I'm afraid or that Sergei is afraid," he said. "We're all just concerned about you."

The boy glared at him, the sharp yelp of his hiccups pulsating in a monotone rhythm. "You're afraid of what I might do. You think I might hurt someone."

"Would you, Vladimir? Would you hurt someone?"

Young Vlad ignored his question. "You're worried that I might grow up to become an evil man. You think I could one day become a murderer."

Suddenly the carriage lurched to a stop. Ilvana Strekov snapped to from her slumber, stretched her arms and let forth a full-body yawn. She wiped the sleep from her eyes and looked around the carriage. The boy was awake, the air in the coach thick with tension.

"What happened here?" she said.

The doctor remained perfectly quiet. Vladimir sat still as well, the sound of his hiccups filling the carriage. The door opened to reveal Tarkov standing outside in the damp air. He lifted Vladimir out of the coach and set the boy down on the wet grass. Alexander joined them. He pulled out his hand-drawn map and examined it in the face of the valley's rolling hills and lime-green vegetation. Alexander discussed their destination briefly with the driver, who pointed to a hill in the far distance.

"The horses are too big for the path," the driver said in broken Russian.

"Where are we going?" Vladimir said.

Alexander crouched down to look Vladimir in the eyes. "You'll find out when we arrive. Now, I don't want any difficulty out of you," he said. "You're going to come with us whether you walk on your own two feet or I have Tarkov here drag you along in the mud."

Vladimir looked up at Tarkov. An absolute mountain of a man, Tarkov folded his arms to reveal thick Herculean biceps bulging under his winter coat. The orderly could crush Vladimir with a single hand. Vladimir gazed off into the distance. He was so far from the unending winter of his village. In every direction there were steep mountains and rolling green hills.

"I suppose he'll have to drag me in the mud," Vladimir said.

Alexander turned to Tarkov. "Pick up the boy," he said. "We must arrive before sundown."

Led by their driver-turned-guide, the Soviets marched through the brush, alternating between muddy jungle paths and grass fields for over an hour before they heard the distant sound of a waterfall. They advanced in the direction of the crashing water until they came to a clearing. In the middle, surrounded by mountains on three sides, was an enormous dwelling with steep arches, its intricate framework laced with ornate carvings and long red cloths. The dwelling stood twelve meters high and three times as wide. A long winding path, lined by small, meticulously aligned bundles of rocks, led up to the entrance. Tarkov set Vladimir down and stared with the others in wonder at this vast structure in the middle of a deserted land.

They approached the front doors. Essentially a series of hollowed-out trees strung together, the doors looked fragile compared to the dwelling's thick, sturdy walls. Shards of light darted out between cracks in the doors, revealing fragments of the room inside. Alexander knocked three times. There was no answer. "Hello," Alexander called, his voice drowned out by the sound of the nearby waterfall. With caution, he pulled on the doors. They flung open to reveal a long, large room, empty save for a lone figure sitting in a chair against the far back wall.

"Enter," the figure said. Alexander ordered the others to remain outside and took Vladimir by the arm. They walked along a thick red carpet toward the figure. The walls were barren as was the ceiling, save for two enormous skylights, one consisting of blue stained glass, the other red. Two beams of incongruent light shone down to cast a nebulous purple glow about the room.

The Russians arrived at the figure. Sitting perfectly erect on an uncomfortable wicker chair was an old Asian man, so tall and rail-thin he would tower over Alexander if he were to stand. The man's head was shaved completely bald and his eyes were closed. His body was covered by a yellow robe. Vladimir had never seen a man so tall. Aside from their guide, he'd never seen a man with such dark skin before either. He glanced up at Alexander, who was quiet as a ghost, waiting for the man to speak.

"Are you Alexander Afiniganov of Russia?" the tall man said in perfect Russian.

"Yes," Alexander said. The doctor's rancorous demeanor had all but vanished. "Are you the Great Gog?"

"I am."

Vladimir hiccupped.

"Does the child always make that sound?" the Great Gog said.

"Yes," Alexander said.

The man looked down at Vladimir and then stood, his legs stretching out like fallen trees rising from the ground. He towered over the Russians. The Great Gog took a long look at the boy. He knelt down on one knee and placed his hand to Vladimir's cheek. Gog looked deep into the young boy's eyes. He stared for a full minute in absolute silence before he stood up again.

"Your fears are well-founded, Alexander Afiniganov of Russia. There is a battle being waged deep within this young one."

"Which battle?"

"The only battle, Doctor — one of good versus evil. Vladimir needs time away from the world to reflect on the child he is and the man he will become. You may leave now. It is time for your party to return home."

"The boy is on a regimen of medication to help him sleep. I can leave you a six-month supply."

"That will not be necessary," the Great Gog said. "Vladimir will no longer need his medication."

Alexander's eyebrow raised. "When should we return to retrieve the child?" he said.

"You must never return for the boy." The Great Gog stepped toward Alexander. "When Vladimir is ready, he will leave on his own."

Alexander had anticipated that the Great Gog would present him with some manner of timetable, an organized method they could use to track the boy's progress either through intermittent visits or correspondence through the post. He looked down at young Vlad and then around the room with its barren walls and hazy lavender light. For the first time, a flicker of doubt resonated in the doctor's mind. What he had done was tantamount to kidnapping. He had no firm idea of Gog's intentions with the boy. Were he to leave Vladimir here and the child happened to never return, there could be a litany of charges back in his homeland — child abduction, abandonment of a minor, crossing the border without proper documentation and, were they to dig deep enough, bribery and the promotion of slavery. What would happen, he wondered, if he turned around and took Vladimir back to Moscow? The answer was nothing. Absolutely nothing would change. The boy would return to Sergei's care, Alexander would be admonished for taking a patient on a trip without permission and Vladimir would continue on his present course, one that Alexander suspected would end tragically amidst an ocean of violence and sorrow.

To Alexander, a man of action and conviction, such a bleak outcome was unacceptable.

"I leave Vladimir in your good care," he said and turned to depart. Alexander walked the long red carpet to where Tarkov and the others were waiting. To his surprise, Vladimir didn't plead with him or beg to return home. The boy stood stone-faced as always. At the door, Alexander waved farewell to the leviathan and the pale child. Young Vlad shot him one last look. It contained not happiness or sorrow, but indignation. Alexander, troubled in his bowels by an obstinate plum he'd consumed during the walk and unsure of himself for the first time, closed the doors and left Vladimir alone with the tall man.

The Great Gog sat down in his hand-woven chair. The wicker splintered and cracked under his weight. With a content sigh, the man closed his eyes and returned to his meditation.

"What now?" Vladimir, standing a meter away, said between yelps.

"My people will rise from their slumber in several hours' time," the Great Gog said without opening his eyes.

"And until then?"

"Until then, we wait."

Vladimir looked around the empty room. Alexander had abandoned him. Sergei would not be coming to save him. The good doctor probably had no idea even where his young patient was. Nor did Vladimir, for that matter. He'd never heard of Mongolia. He didn't know if he was still in Russia or if he'd been taken to the other side of the world. And, despite all their fears, he was still a child. Left alone in this foreign place, with the spectral purple light shining down from above and the tall man having forgotten he was in the room, Vladimir did the only thing he could do — he stood there waiting, his hiccups filling the silence every 3.7 seconds.

He was now at the mercy of the Great Gog.

Part
Two

eight

Mongolia, 1941

The water pummeled down from above. Thousands of shards of ice pierced Vladimir's skin like tiny daggers. In his shoulder blades, deep incisions formed. Vladimir felt his temperature drop the moment he entered the waterfall. It was so dense he could stretch his arms to their full width and still not touch the air. Vladimir faltered under the torrent from above. Never before had the terror of dying been so immediate. It was a sensation like no other.

Thirty minutes before, Vladimir — a young man now, twenty years old, strong with a thick, sturdy frame and capable of growing a long beard — approached the doors at the entrance of Gog's temple. Vladimir hadn't seen the hazy purple light inside for months, ever since Gog banished him. In that time he haunted the monastery like a ghost that no one ever saw. Vladimir lived in the trees. He took shelter in a secluded cave a kilometer away. When he was hungry, he ate. When he was thirsty, he drank. The rest of his time was spent practicing his skills as a hunter. Vladimir's condition put him at a severe disadvantage. His hiccups announced his presence before he could catch his prey by surprise. Through sheer determination and cunning, he managed to capture animal after animal until there was not one manner of mammal, bird or lizard that he had not held in his hands.

Vladimir had reached physical maturation, and still the tortured, jangled collection of thoughts stormed about his mind. Still they pushed violently toward the front of his skull. At times Vladimir's year in the jungle bordered on sheer lunacy. He had taken to hunting animals as if they were humans. Vladimir would picture men, women, even children, as he stalked his prey through the wild, the glistening tip of a spear raised high above, a wild zeal encompassing him. After Vladimir made the kill, he would retreat to his cave and scream at the top of his lungs for hours. He spent days stumbling aimlessly through the brush, holding his hands to his head, panicked, with tears streaming down his face.

Now he returned to Gog — Gog, who in all these years had taught him nothing. Not civility or honor or passion or even arithmetic or how to cook rice. Gog, who was a monument, worshiped by his followers like a statue constructed millennia ago. Vladimir could count on his fingers the number of times Gog had spoken to him over the years. He dreaded going back. But he couldn't live in the wild anymore. Vladimir had become a prisoner in his own mind and he had to return while he still maintained some semblance of control.

It was the middle of the afternoon on a chilly mid-autumn's day. The grass was frosted. Even the bright sun wasn't enough to warm the air. Vladimir entered through the doors of the long room uninvited. Every few steps he emitted the sound of a frog's ribbit. The Great Gog seemed not to notice. He was sitting perfectly erect in his wicker chair as always, his eyes closed, a faded monument in this empty, forsaken room.

Vladimir knew Gog had the ability to hear during even the deepest of trances. He walked straight up to the tall man.

"Gog?" he said.

There was no answer.

"Gog?"

The old warrior sat perfectly still. Vladimir waited in the purple light for Gog to release a long, pensive breath. It never came. He reached out and touched Gog's face. The tall man's skin was as cold as the air outside. "Gog?" He grabbed the leviathan by the shoulders and shook him. "Speak!" he cried.

Like an oak tree being felled, Gog toppled over. Vladimir stepped out of the way and Gog landed in an unceremonious heap on the floor. In the distance, Gog's followers entered through the hollow doors. Vladimir knew how this looked: the hiccupping child, a white devil standing over top of their fallen messiah. He stared straight through them. Almost immediately the followers disavowed their silence and yelled at Vladimir in their native Buryat dialect. Vladimir braced himself for what was about to come.

In the waterfall, the night destroyed the day. And not just the night but the end of all days, the absence of places and people and things. Blackness forced its way up from the ground, the heavens collapsed and all around was the sensation of liquid. Liquid land, liquid air. Vladimir's flesh felt malleable, dissolved. He existed but he did not exist. He could think and feel and understand the world around him but trust in nothing.

Gog's followers were on him like a plague of locusts. They attacked Vladimir from all sides, their sudden vengeful fury shocking, considering the peace in which they'd lived. Vladimir struggled to defend himself. He fell to the floor amidst an onslaught of legs and fists, his only defense to curl himself into a ball and shield his organs with his limbs.

Minutes later, he felt himself being dragged up the mountain toward the Waterfall of Ion. Not since Vladimir's first month in Mongolia had a man entered the waterfall, and that man, Tomchar, did not survive. The power of the icy water had overwhelmed Gog's ambitious follower; it gushed and streamed its relentless force. Tomchar slipped. His head crashed into the limestone and his lifeless body cascaded into the rocks below. Gog — whose legend was established when he withstood the waterfall's fury — forbade his followers from ever entering the Waterfall of Ion again.

Vladimir screamed. He struggled in vain. The sound next to the water was staggering. Vladimir couldn't hear himself anymore. Without ceremony or discussion, they cast him inside.

★ ★ ★

For so long Vladimir's perspective had been distorted, bent to serve the thundering storms inside his mind. Evil is not only powerful, not just alluring — it's knowing, it's aware. From the first moment he had awoken in the hospital in Moscow, Vladimir knew his role in this world was to be a scourge on all mankind. He would kill hundreds, thousands even. Millions if he had the means. The doctors poked him, they prodded him, they cast him aside into the land of lunatics and still he knew. He kept it in his ever-present vacuous glare.

★ ✳ ★

Imprinted forever on Vladimir's mind was the look of dread on Markus's face. When he finally spoke to that self-proclaimed practitioner of the brain, what emerged? Even Vladimir himself could not be certain. Was it a sinuous arrangement of jagged thoughts and emotions so utterly raw, so very base, that they set a plague upon the room? Or had Vladimir known exactly what he was doing and fallen victim to his own cleverness?

He'd seen through Markus, of that he was sure. As Markus lobbed question upon question into the air over multiple sessions in a futile attempt to make Vladimir talk, a pattern emerged. Markus was — and of this fact Vladimir had never been more certain — deathly afraid of his older brother. The questions Markus asked, the labored syllables that lurched off the tip of his tongue when he mentioned family, responsibility, brotherhood and obligation, spoke volumes. Vladimir waited, serpent-like in the weeds, until he was ready. Then he pounced. He attacked. He twisted Markus's words, contorted them until they were both potent and unrecognizable.

Had he meant it when he told Markus that he didn't love Ileana? No. Of course not. Even now, as the water crashed around him, he wanted nothing more than to see Ileana again, the profile of her face, enchanting and pure. But he would never tell Markus that, he would never even tell Sergei. He was then not even ten years old. And he had much work to do.

★ ✳ ★

Now the waterfall raged. Vladimir's demise was a certainty, like the spinning of the Earth or the rising of the sun. He would meet his end here, and for the first time in his life he was afraid. His murderous aspirations abandoned him like a plague of rats streaming off a sinking ship. He lifted his hand and the waterfall pummeled him back down. Vladimir brought his shoulder blades up and was forced into the limestone by a wall of ice.

Was it not Alexander Afiniganov's plan for Vladimir to leave Mongolia a good man, a better man — reformed and matured? Why then did Gog leave Vladimir to his own devices? And where was his mother? Where was his long-lost father? Where were Sergei and Alexander while he stood under the waterfall with those who meant to kill him lurking outside?

Abandoned and left for dead, Vladimir looked within. What he found, what Vladimir clung to, what had defined him and separated him from lunacy all along, were his hiccups, the one part of his life that had never abandoned him. They'd become his constant companion, his security, an internal clock ticking with the regularity of a perfectly balanced pendulum. Vladimir had always hidden himself in their warmth. In the end, as the waterfall beat him down, the hiccups became the perfect cicerone. Their stamina and fortitude guided Vladimir to the realization that sometimes in life, the person you are is the person you decide to be.

Vladimir raised a single knee. Still the water raged. He raised his left hand and then the other. Vladimir lifted his chin and opened his eyes. The water forced them closed, but in that moment he saw light. Vladimir saw the world as it existed: true, organic, a story yet unwritten. That plague in his core, the one that had festered for so many years, lost its sense of predetermination. Vladimir could move, he could feel, he could breathe and, most important of all, he could decide. Vladimir raised his arms. He screamed. Water swirled in his mouth. He spat it out and screamed again. Vladimir twirled around inside the waterfall now — slowly but with confidence. He opened his eyes. Vladimir cast Gog's followers a final glare. The hiccupping boy, now a man, turned and dove out from the Waterfall of Ion into the distant pool below.

nine

The next day, before Gog's followers cleared out of the monastery, one of them presented Vladimir with a small box. Inside was a handwritten note in Russian. It read:

> *Have you found your peace, Vladimir?*
> *Have you chosen your path?*
> *Yes, you have. I always knew you would. Gog.*

Vladimir smiled when he read the note. He set it aside and searched through the rest of the box. Inside was an envelope containing both Mongolian and Russian currency. It was more than enough to pay for Vladimir's passage anywhere he wanted to go. Underneath the Mongolian tugriks and Russian rubles was a compass and, beside that, a detailed map of their current location along with directions for how Vladimir could reach the border. At the top of the map, in the left corner, Gog had drawn a large red circle around the city of Moscow.

It took a full day after crossing the Russian-Mongolian border before Vladimir found a road. The long dirt and gravel expanse traveled northeast, and while Gog's map directed him due north, Vladimir chose to walk along the road, no matter what detour it caused. After two weeks of traversing the rolling green hills of Mongolia, he had started to feel hemmed in by the endless fields of grass. The open world, the absence of people and things, the indefinable sense of place where everything around him was lush and green, became claustrophobic with time. Vladimir might as well have been trapped on a desert island, a three-by-five-meter area of sand with a single palm tree, as walking alone through these fields.

He turned onto the rural road and kept marching, secretly hoping to meet a person along the way, someone, anyone, to remind him of the civilized world. Vladimir's salvation came in the form of a horse-drawn wagon. He saw it from a kilometer away. Vladimir thought it might be a mirage, a dream of some sort. The closer the wagon drew, the firmer the edges of its outline, the more apparent the discolored brown of the horse and the thick, bald head of the farmer steering the wagon, the more Vladimir realized this was not a dream. His imagination — he was sure — would have conjured up something more appealing than a tall, muscular farmer of late middle age with a jaw covered in long-healed acne scars and boils on his temples and neck.

As they neared, the farmer stepped off his wagon. He reached back onto the flatbed and produced a pitchfork, then brandished the weapon at Vladimir.

"Are you a soldier?" he said.

Vladimir stared straight through him, stunned. It had been so long since Vladimir heard someone speak the Russian language.

"Are you Japanese? Are you a soldier? Do you have a weapon?"

The farmer's words entered Vladimir's ears and traveled the long-unused auricular neural pathways of his brain. It took a few moments, but like a series of pipes being cleared of debris, the passageways slowly retook their familiar shape and Vladimir understood what the farmer was saying.

"I'm Russian," he said.

The farmer poked the pitchfork in the air. "Prove it."

"How?" Vladimir said.

"Sing the anthem. Sing 'The Internationale.'"

Vladimir scratched his head. He racked his brain for the melody to a song he hadn't heard in over ten years. "I don't remember exactly how it goes," he said.

"Then you're not Russian."

"It has something to do with a final struggle. Grouping together to form a human race."

The farmer waved the pitchfork in the air again. "Sing it!" he yelled.

Vladimir looked back at the limitless expanse of green fields. He could undoubtedly outrun this man. The farmer was at least twenty-five years older than Vladimir, maybe as many as thirty. His huge biceps and powerful shoulders would only hinder him in an all-out sprint. But was this how Vladimir wanted to reintroduce himself to society? By turning and running from the first sign of trouble he encountered?

He gathered his words as best he could and then — absent any redeemable melody — sang what he remembered of "The Internationale." The sound was ghastly. Vladimir knew it even as it exited his mouth. He could barely carry a tune and every time he felt he was gaining momentum, a hiccup would emerge from the back of his throat. The farmer's expression turned more peculiar with each involuntary yelp. Eventually he lowered his pitchfork and put his hand in the air, the universal symbol for an aspiring vocalist to immediately conclude an audition gone awry.

"What's that sound?"

"I have the hiccups. It's been almost twelve years now."

"Strange," the farmer said. "Very strange." He paused. "Are you looking for a ride?" he said.

"I'm headed back to Moscow," Vladimir said.

The farmer stared off into the distance. "That's quite a long way. You might think of taking a train."

"My plan exactly. I'm journeying first to Irkutsk." He held his map up in his hand. "There I intend to book passage west-ward on the Trans-Siberian railway."

"Going back the way you came?"

"More or less."

The farmer tossed his pitchfork into the back of his empty wagon. He climbed up and took the horse's reins. "I'm going to Irkutsk on business in three days' time." He took a long look at Vladimir. "I could use a young man like you around the farm. If you're willing to work hard for a few days, I'll take you straight into Irkutsk. We'll even take my automobile, travel in high style. Does that seem like a fair exchange to you, boy?"

Vladimir nodded. The farmer motioned for him to climb aboard and Vladimir hopped up with his satchel in hand. They started traveling along the road in the direction from which Vladimir had just come. Vladimir said his name. He reached out to shake the man's hand. The farmer just grunted and took Vladimir's hand in his. "My name's Usurpet," he said, his eyes locked on the road. It was thirty minutes later, after they'd circled through a valley and out the other side, when Usurpet spoke again. "I thought you were a soldier."

"A Russian soldier?" Vladimir said.

"Maybe. Meeting a Russian soldier along this stretch of road wouldn't be all that bad. Though even one of our own can't be trusted these days."

"I don't understand," Vladimir said. "Who else would it be? Is the Mongolian army attacking the Soviet South?"

Usurpet shot Vladimir a curious look. "You don't know about the Germans? About the war?"

"I've been away a long time," he said.

"How long?"

"Ten years."

Usurpet shook his head. "We're at war, boy! The Great Patriotic War has been waging for well over two years now. Germany and Hitler have invaded Russia. They're in the north and they approach the south. Just last year the Japanese attacked Russia through the East Mongolian border." Usurpet paused. "How did you get past the border?"

Vladimir shrugged his shoulders. He showed Usurpet his map. "I followed the directions here. I didn't see any soldiers or any border guards. I just walked through a series of grass fields, each greener than the last, until I came upon this road."

Usurpet pulled on the horse's reins, forcing the wagon to come to an abrupt halt. He gazed at Vladimir, watched the hiccups pulse out of the young man's mouth and turned his bald head to the side until his entire body formed a question mark. "You're the luckiest fool I've ever met. These fields are teeming with enemy soldiers. Even now as we speak, the Germans advance on Moscow. They practically own the south. Thousands of Russian soldiers are dying every day. If that isn't all we have to worry about, the Japanese are still here. Their army stagnated in the Mongolian deserts but some of them slipped through. There've been sightings; I know it for a fact. The Japanese army left behind dozens of soldiers, dangerous armed men scattered across the south, now cut off from any communication with their generals. They've been trolling the fields for random villages to plunder. I haven't let my wife or daughter off my property in over a year. It's not safe. The world isn't safe."

"What about the railway?" Vladimir said. "Will I still be able to book passage?"

Usurpet nodded. "As far as I know. You might have trouble getting close to Moscow, but here in the east, the railways are still functioning as normal." He thrashed the reins and the horse started up again.

Usurpet steered the wagon off the main road straight into a grass field and past an assemblage of tall oak trees. They traveled deeper into the woods, where the smell became a hodgepodge of decaying tree bark and freshly cut nepeta mint plants, before coming upon a clearing. Usurpet's home was a bungalow of sorts, not attached to any road or township as far as Vladimir could see. His dwelling stood in front of a white barn situated next to a steep ravine and behind that, fields of crops. It was just as Usurpet had described it. Safe. Hidden. Ramshackle.

Usurpet led Vladimir out back of the barn and let him wash up in a barrel of gelid rainwater. Once Vladimir had wiped his armpits and face, and cleaned his nether regions with a rag, Usurpet led him inside the bungalow, where his wife and teenage daughter were preparing dinner. He barked a few words at the women and then motioned for Vladimir to sit next to him in front of the fireplace. Usurpet threw a log on the pile of burning embers and leaned back in his chair. Bright orange sparks settled in the air. On the wall directly above Usurpet, the upper torso and head of a mounted bear stared directly at Vladimir, its eyes glassy and white.

"You'll have to excuse my wife," Usurpet said. "We haven't had visitors in two years, ever since the war started in Europe. You're the first man besides me to set foot in this house in a long time."

Vladimir looked at Usurpet's wife in the distance.

"She can't speak," Usurpet said. "Something was wrong with her throat when she was a girl." His wife walked by and cast a look at the two men sitting by the inglenook. She received a swift slap on the buttocks from Usurpet for her troubles. "The boy's hungry," he said and turned his attention back to Vladimir.

"A question for you," Vladimir said. "You explained the war during our journey."

"Was there something wrong with my telling of it?"

"No, of course not. There are just a few things I don't understand. For instance, can you tell me again the difference between a Nazi and a kamikaze?"

Usurpet exhaled a half chuckle, half groan of exhaustion. "A Nazi is a German soldier. They belong to a political movement, an extreme brand of socialism. The kamikazes are Japanese soldiers, pilots by trade. They aim their planes into Soviet ships and buildings with the intent to kill everyone aboard and themselves as well."

"So these Nazis," Vladimir said, "do they fly their planes straight into crowds of Jewish people?"

"No. They're committing genocide."

"I'm not familiar with that word."

"They're killing the Jews. All of them. Women and children too. I hear they've killed thousands of Polish people as well."

"Why?" Vladimir said.

"What do you mean, why?"

"Why don't the Germans like the Jews?"

"Because the Jews murdered and tortured Jesus Christ," Usurpet said.

"But that was a thousand years ago."

"Two thousand, actually."

Vladimir paused. "That seems like an enormously long time to hold a grudge."

"People don't forget," Usurpet said.

"Then what about the Polish? Why are the Nazis killing them?"

Usurpet shuffled in his seat. He glanced back at his wife and daughter and told them dinner had better be ready soon. Usurpet picked up a fire poker and, much as he handled the pitchfork earlier, jabbed the log atop the fire until tiny red fireflies danced in the air. "At our core, humankind is driven by our quest for power," he said. "Simple men like you and me, farmers and boot makers and day laborers, have become few and far between. This is the year 1941. The industrial revolution is well behind us. The Eastern War with Britain and Sardinia is almost a hundred years past. In America, capitalism breeds like a virus. The world — Europe and the Americas at least — is there for the taking. And every man — Hitler included — wants to be the next Count Suvorov of Rymnik."

"I'm afraid I don't know who that is," Vladimir said.

Usurpet scrunched his nose in disgust. "In order to be a proud Soviet, Vladimir, you must know of the proud Soviets who came before you. Suvorov is the most famous Russian general of all time. He destroyed the Turks. He decimated the Ottoman Empire. He never failed in battle, not even once! All of these men, Stalin and Hitler and Churchill, can only dream of the glory Suvorov achieved."

A small, almost tender voice sounded from the kitchen. "Father," Usurpet's daughter said. "It's time for dinner."

Usurpet ignored her. "The world is at a precipice," he said. "At the turn of the century, men had never seen tanks before. Now they're commonplace. Airplanes drop liquid fire from the sky. The Japanese hate us. The Chinese fear us. The Americans cannot be trusted. And the Germans march about with their chins held high like drunken louts leaving a tavern in search of a fight. Russia — as we know it — might end up in ashes." He poked the fire again. "Men like us must never lose sight of who we are. The mettle of a Russian man's soul is carved not in wood but in stone." Usurpet leaned forward. The flames flickered in the whites of his eyes. "I, for one, will die before I allow my great country to be burned to the ground."

Vladimir watched Usurpet during the meal. The farmer was a messy eater — he stabbed his knife haphazardly, without precision, seemingly without forethought, into the bulk or length of the side of beef loin he intended to divide. He gnashed his teeth as well. Usurpet's yellow incisors exploded up and down; the muttony mixture of meat and carrots collided about in his open mouth like a small anguished creature trying to escape an ancient Romanian killing machine. All the while, as he poked furiously at his potatoes with a three-pronged trident of a fork, Usurpet's eyes gazed soft and serene at his daughter.

His only child, with lush copper hair and gray, almost silver-tinged eyes, Karadine had yet to turn sixteen. Usurpet watched her at all times. His eyes locked onto her, they melted into her, were drawn to her as though she were the only

source of light in a darkened room. Vladimir paid close attention. Usurpet's left eye, the one without the lazy inclination of
the pupil, and even the eye that at times refused to function
— they claimed her for his very own. Vladimir could only
imagine Usurpet's pain. If only he lived in a different time, an
ancient time in which Electra carnality was lawful, expected,
even encouraged, it would be Usurpet's paternal responsibility
to bring his daughter into womanhood. He could do so safely,
serenely, gently. But this was modern Russia and Usurpet was
this girl's father. That was his curse. He could never seek more
than but the most chaste kiss on her forehead, never unhinge
her in the manner in which kings unhinged their daughters
millennia ago, never truly bury himself in her warmth. Damn
any unwashed lout who even tried.

Usurpet's eyes swung toward Vladimir. It was him they
impaled, him they shot straight through. *You dare not touch
her. You dare not approach her virginal womanhood, you hiccupping fiend!* Vladimir looked down at his thick, bloody cut of
meat. He buried his head in his plate and shoveled his food
in without complaint, secretly hoping for the evening to end
and for the solace of the soft and crunchy bed of hay in the
barn Usurpet had promised. He'd almost finished his carrots
and a good portion of his beef — Vladimir could only specu-
late from the degree of fatty tissue, its stringiness and preva-
lence of veins strewn throughout, that this particular piece
came from either a cow's lower shin or the creature's neck —
when he felt a strange sensation under the table. Something
was crawling up his pant leg. Vladimir twitched in his seat. It
might have been a spider. Or perhaps even a mouse. Vladimir
shook his foot. He shook it again, vigorously this time. He
was about to stand up when he looked over and saw Usurpet's
wife curl her mouth into an ophidian smile.

It was the farmer's wife, the mute woman with a slightly round face and a bawdy display of bosom. Her toe, the tip of her stocking, crawled up and down Vladimir's leg like a coiled finger. It slid ever so gently along his shin bone, stopped to cup itself around the side of his calf muscle and then relinquished its hold only to slither up and down again. Vladimir glanced over at Usurpet. That pointed fork remained menacingly in his grasp; his mouth continued to wreak havoc on anything thrust within its confines. His eyes locked on Karadine's chest and how it rose and fell with each breath, how her dress clung to her like a veil, the beauty in her face as the flickering candlelight revealed its absence of shadows. The wife's toe climbed up Vladimir's leg again. It lifted past his knee and traveled toward his inner thigh.

Vladimir finished his last bite.

He took a swift gulp from his tankard of ale.

"Finished," he said.

Usurpet looked at him. His wife and daughter stared as well. Vladimir hiccupped. Three-point-seven seconds passed and he hiccupped again.

Usurpet stood up. He shoveled his last two bites into his mouth and then stomped away from the table. From an adjacent bedroom, Usurpet fetched a pillow and two blankets. He lumbered out the front door without a word. Vladimir looked at the two women — Karadine, whose eyes never drifted from her meal, and Usurpet's wife with her coy smile. The wife leaned back in her chair. Her plentiful bosom rose toward the rafters. Vladimir wasn't sure, but he could have sworn that as she looked at him — eyes locked like a serpent's — her legs drifted ever so slightly apart. She said nothing, this middle-aged muted minx, just stared as Vladimir backed toward the door.

"Good evening to you ladies," he said and took his leave.

It was already night outside. Vladimir found Usurpet some thirty paces ahead of him, walking toward the small white barn behind the house. He jogged to catch up and joined Usurpet just as the farmer opened the barn door. Its hinges creaked loudly. The barn smelled exactly as Vladimir had anticipated. Not pleasant but not so disagreeable that he would be unable to get a full night's sleep. There was no livestock in attendance, no stray chickens or gaunt, unkempt goats milling about. Just a slight odor to remember their presence. Usurpet lit a lantern near the front and pointed to a ladder and a loft some four meters in the air.

"You'll find the straw up there. It's quite comfortable. There's enough room for six or seven men," he said and handed Vladimir the pillow and blankets. "Tomorrow we wake at sunrise. The fields need work. Maybe there'll be time to slaughter a pig. We'll see what the day brings."

Usurpet turned and left. He shut the door behind him.

"Good night," Vladimir said.

He gazed around. The light from the lantern by the door had gone out and Vladimir had to wait for his eyes to adjust to the dark. In the roof, gaps had formed alongside the individual boards that didn't match up to their adjacent planks of wood, allowing the blue moonlight to trickle through. Stygian cobwebs dangled from the rafters like a chambermaid's abandoned lacework. The entire place looked haunted, like a devilish dwelling in a storybook from Vladimir's youth. Vladimir half expected some vile and deranged quadruped to lurch out of a nearby haystack and swipe at him with a crooked dagger, half expected voices to call up from the floorboards, trying to convince him that Usurpet kept a dozen victims down below, haggard and barely alive: not victims — slaves really. *You'll be next,* they would say. *Guard yourself, Vladimir, flee this place immediately. Not tomorrow, not the next day or an hour from now. Get out now while you're still a free man, unshackled, not one of Usurpet's captive chattel.*

Vladimir shook his head. The dark was playing tricks on his mind. Usurpet was a farmer, a simple workingman. Nothing more. Vladimir climbed the wooden ladder and found the bed of hay above. There was a window up in the loft. He could have closed it. He could have shut out the cold of night. But as he lay in bed and wrapped both blankets around his torso, Vladimir enjoyed looking out into the stars. The evening sky was clear. Vladimir thought of his mother to the north, his doctors Alexander Afiniganov and Sergei Namestikov to the west. Ileana, that angelic young creature from his village's schoolhouse. As he'd done so many nights while in the company of Gog, Vladimir gazed up into the stars and imagined them looking into the same night sky. He leaned back and let the hay envelop him, closed his eyes and focused on his breathing. It took no more than three minutes for Vladimir to fade peacefully into sleep.

Hours later — or was it minutes? The night sky betrayed no hint of the time — Vladimir was awoken by a sudden loud creak. Down below, moonlight shone through a crack in the barn doors. Someone had entered. Vladimir heard footsteps shuffle soft and quiet below. The floorboards shifted. Vladimir knew before he even saw her who it was. Usurpet's wife. That mute woman with the beckoning eyes. He swallowed a deep breath. She was climbing the ladder now, only a few steps away. Vladimir sat upright. He thought of the woman's plentiful cleavage, how her toes toyed with him, the pout in her eyes. How angry Usurpet would be. How his rage would boil over if he came upon them. Vladimir made up his mind before she even finished climbing the ladder. He would send her away. There were other conquests to be had in this world, notwithstanding the wife of a muscular farmer, particularly a man who owned and often vigorously operated a pitchfork.

Then a strange sight appeared. In the outline of moonlight from below popped the head of Usurpet's daughter, Karadine. Beautiful and pale in the faint moonlight, she put a single finger to her lips. "Shhh," she said. Vladimir hiccupped. He closed his mouth to hold them at bay. Surely she couldn't expect him to suppress them entirely. Karadine climbed up onto the loft. She sat beside him, that thin finger still pressed to her mouth. Her transparent nightdress revealed tight, small nipples pointing upward on her pert breasts. Vladimir felt flush. His blood turned warm. She edged closer, brought her hand from her mouth to his.

"Shhh," she said again. Karadine slid her fingers to the base of his jaw and slipped her warm wet tongue inside Vladimir's parted lips. She pulled her nightdress off her shoulder. Vladimir reached out and, for the first time since infanthood, he cupped a breast in his hand. It was softer than he expected, yet somehow much firmer as well. He never wanted to let go. Karadine was still kissing him — her lips sodden with wine and the taste of mint — when Vladimir hiccupped straight into her mouth. He half expected her to recoil in horror. Karadine smiled instead. She pulled herself up and slipped out of the nightdress. It descended her body slowly, as though the very fabric knew how fortunate it was to be wrapped around her unvarnished beauty; it clung to her stomach, and Karadine had to reach down, shift her hips and slip out of the nightdress entirely to reveal the taut, ivory flesh of her naked body. She fell gently to her knees and smiled again, locked eyes with Vladimir and released a girlish giggle, then leaned forward to undo his belt. Karadine pulled his pants down to his knees and prepared to climb atop him.

At that very moment, the barn door creaked again.

A look of terror shot through Karadine's eyes.

"Father!" she whispered and scrambled about in frantic search of her nightdress. In her panic, Karadine couldn't find it in the moonlight. She went to stand up when Vladimir grabbed her wrist.

"Usurpet will see you." He motioned her down.

"He owns a shotgun," she said. Then she scurried into the corner on her hands and knees and began burying herself in the straw. Vladimir pleaded with her. He whispered over and over again, "This isn't a good plan. You have to get down from here, you have to flee." But the girl wouldn't listen. She kept tossing straw on top of her naked body until she was entirely concealed. Vladimir heard footsteps below, heavier this time, not like Karadine's. He looked out the window. The loft was situated too far up, the hillside next to the barn too steep to risk the jump. His pants were still down around his knees. The wood shifted on the ladder. Usurpet was climbing up, undoubtedly with his shotgun. Vladimir panicked. He reached forward, grabbed the girl's nightdress and tossed it into the center of the barn. Only as the sheer fabric sailed through the air did he realize it would have been much wiser to hurl the evidence out the open window. Vladimir reached down to pull up his pants when a face appeared at the top of the ladder.

It wasn't the farmer Usurpet.

It was his wife.

The farmer's wife sashayed up the last few steps and climbed toward Vladimir just as her daughter had done a minute ago. Only this time Vladimir was stark naked from the waist down. The wife's mouth opened in shock. She looked at Vladimir's erect penis and then up at his eyes and back down again. Vladimir glanced to his side. The haystack hadn't moved. It refused to even shift with the girl's breath. He looked back at the farmer's wife. Her expression of shock had been replaced by one of warm-blooded glee. She was wearing a nightdress as well, this one short and red. It dangled around her hips to reveal nothing on her bottom. She crawled forward and put her finger to her mouth just as Karadine had done. Only this time, Vladimir wasn't sure whether to propel a scream of joy or bellow in revolt. The wife launched herself upon him. Vladimir hiccupped. The haystack remained motionless. The farmer's wife was positioning herself. She squatted, her hips wide, the mass of her buttocks double the size of Vladimir's own. He put his hands up to push her away, but his resistance came too late.

The moment Usurpet's wife sat her proud, wide vagina upon his penis, Vladimir exploded. His loins erupted in a sudden burst of carnal release. Vladimir's orgasm was profound, it was liberating, it flowed like a shooting river all the way from his feet, up through his knees, into his thighs, and then finally, in its purest form, a quick outpouring of sticky white goo. Vladimir grunted and coughed; he hiccupped again. Usurpet's wife looked shocked once more. That shock quickly morphed into a look of disappointment. She made a noise, one that only the mute make, an echo in her throat that never escaped her mouth. Vladimir could tell from her eyes and the way her hands cupped around his face exactly what it meant — *That's okay, dear. We'll try again in a couple of minutes.*

"Karadine?"

A man's voice sounded from the barn door.

A match broke into flame and lit the lantern by the door.

Vladimir heaved the woman aside and pulled up his pants.

"Karadine?" the voice said again. "I know you're in here. Vladimir, you better not be doing what I think you're doing."

Vladimir poked his head over the railing. There was Usurpet, brandishing a lantern in one hand and a shotgun in the other. He pointed the shotgun toward Vladimir.

Vladimir ducked. He considered once again leaping into the ravine below.

"You little bastard! You get down here with my daughter!"

"She's not up here," Vladimir yelled back. He glanced over at that unmoving pile of hay again. If Usurpet saw Karadine, Vladimir was sure to receive a bullet between his eyes. He looked at Usurpet's wife, who was still bristling with disappointment. She moved to stand up. Vladimir considered stopping her. He even went so far as to reach out to grab one of her supple, meaty thighs. He stopped himself at the last moment and turned around instead, making ready to jump from the window into the ravine below.

Usurpet's wife waved to her husband. Upon seeing his spouse in her nightgown, her bottom portion nude, her hair a mess — although that was no matter; his wife's hair had long been a constant source of tangles, a veritable breeding ground of lice — Usurpet uttered a curse in Russian and then unexpectedly began to laugh. His laugh built from its initial chortle into a full-blown convulsion of hilarity. Vladimir, perched at the window, and at that very moment attempting to choose the landing spot least likely to break both his ankles, paused. Usurpet called out his name. In between laughs he called out again.

Cautiously, Vladimir peered over the ledge and looked down at Usurpet. The man had set his gun down on the wooden floor. He was still laughing so hard it was difficult for him to stand up straight. "Why didn't you say so, my boy? All you had to do was ask."

Vladimir looked over at Usurpet's wife. Her expression of disappointment had magnified a hundred times over.

"Come down," Usurpet said. "Come down and talk to me, boy."

Still cautious, Vladimir grabbed his satchel and descended the ladder. The farmer's wife followed right behind him. They stood before the husband, a man betrayed. The lantern light danced in his hand with each consecutive full-bodied laugh. Usurpet reached out his heavily calloused fingers and placed them on Vladimir's shoulder. He calmed himself down as best he could.

"My wife is a grown woman. She can bed whomever she chooses," he said.

Usurpet looked over at his wife. These words seemed to soften her expression slightly.

"I'll be taking my leave," Usurpet said. He turned back and bent over to pick up his shotgun when suddenly he stopped. Usurpet walked five paces toward the wall, reached down and pulled something from the dust. He put his nose to it, breathed in the fabric fully and completely, then turned and shook the nightdress in the air.

"Karadine!" he bellowed. "Karadine, where are you?!"

Vladimir started to edge his way toward the barn doors.

"Karadine!" Usurpet yelled again. His face had turned red, a thick pulsing vein bulging from the skin above his eyebrows. The vein oscillated, throbbed, like a frantic snake slithering within Usurpet's forehead. Vladimir took two more steps backward. He was within a meter of the doorway now. Usurpet pointed an accusing finger. "Don't you move, boy!" Vladimir prepared himself for the full fury of the farmer's rage when from above a vision appeared.

It was Karadine, that beautiful girl of fifteen, naked and white against the backdrop of moonlight. She stood at the precipice of the loft, her toes curled over the edge, tiny fragments of straw drifting from her body, and stared down at her mother and father. Usurpet, who had long coveted the moment he would see her blossom into womanhood, stood still and amazed. His face had the look of a drunkard who, after years at the drink — his liver failing, skin yellowing in the sickness that followed — had taken to the bottle for one final night of self-destructive revelry and now stood awash in a muddled and half-crocked state, defiant and filled with joy. There was Karadine, his Karadine, naked and full in her womanhood. Oh, how he pined for her. How he'd longed for this day.

Vladimir edged farther toward the door. He'd almost taken his leave.

Usurpet's expression changed to one of profound sorrow. "My little girl," he mouthed without making a sound.

Karadine pointed her finger at Vladimir. "He made me do it, Papa," she said. "He made us both do it."

Usurpet turned toward Vladimir. His eyes formed flaming-red spheres. The farmer dropped his lantern. His shotgun still lay at the center of the floor. Vladimir canceled his retreat. He and Usurpet both eyed the gun, then each other. Vladimir was eight paces away, maybe as many as nine. Usurpet was only four. In a sudden move, Usurpet lunged to the floor and picked up the shotgun. Vladimir turned and ran. He took off into the dark of night. Vladimir was five meters into the field when he heard the first shotgun blast. He kept running, one hand on his satchel, the other arm pumping in the air. The farmer cried out his name. A second blast fired and Vladimir fell to the ground. Unharmed, he pulled himself up again and ran; the shotgun fired once more and he kept running. His hiccups choked in his chest, but Vladimir didn't stop until the dark gave way to the dawn and he was several kilometers away.

Vladimir looked back for the hundredth time. There was no sign of Usurpet behind him, no sign of the farmer's horse and wagon. It was then and only then that Vladimir collapsed, almost unwillingly, into a thorny patch of rose bushes and closed his exhausted eyes.

ten

Three days later, Vladimir approached the township of Kyakhta, the last landmark on Gog's map leading to the large Siberian city of Irkutsk and its railway. As Gog had advised, he trekked over a small mountain — a hill really, compared to the daunting height of the towering peaks in the distance. The morning following Usurpet's attempted vengeance and murder, Vladimir had slept for several hours next to the thicket of rose bushes and then moved on, wary of any roadways that Usurpet might be patrolling with pitchfork in hand. He could clearly visualize a scene in which Karadine and her mute mother stood on the back of Usurpet's wagon, spotting scopes in their hands, trolling the hillside, with Usurpet lashing away at his horse from his seat on the wooden cart. Vladimir stayed to the countryside. When he was hungry, he hunted. He fashioned a makeshift spear and slew — in order — a partridge, two cranes, a five-toed pygmy and a snowy owl. He cooked the pygmy and the fowl over a fire during the daylight hours so as not to be discovered. Vladimir was also fortunate enough to come upon an apple tree at the edge of a farmer's plantation and fill his satchel to the point of bursting.

Now he'd come to the final township before Lake Baikal and could avoid human contact no longer. Autumn had set in weeks ago and the chill in the air, the lack of give to the ground beneath him, the icy dew covering the earth in the morning, spoke of a fast-approaching winter. Lake Baikal was a large body of water, surrounded by mountains. Vladimir didn't have time to walk all the way around the lake to reach Irkutsk. His feet hurt. Large blisters had formed on three of his toes, another one at the base of his heel. He needed to stop and rest. He needed at least one night's sleep in a warm bed before finding his way over the mountains and across the lake. He would need to barter passage.

The town square in Kyakhta was crowded with people, traders mostly, some bartering with their Chinese counterparts, others displaying their wares. Furs, teas and fruits, live cattle and leather products, candles, rhubarb and porcelain. The teeming mass in the square moved like a single unwashed organism, an odor of sour milk and dried sweat wafting from their bodies.

The first individual Vladimir came into contact with was a small boy, perhaps as young as four years old. He had one blackened front tooth and wore a stained coat made of rabbit fur. The boy begged for some spare change. He looked up at Vladimir with pleading eyes, his little face covered in soot. Vladimir reached into his satchel and pulled out a single kopeck. He placed it in the child's hand. Before he walked two more steps, another child reached out his poor little hand. Then another and another. Vladimir found himself surrounded by eight of these misbegotten orphans, each older than the last, some nearly equal his height. Their reaching hands grabbed at his bag, and what had begun so simply as an act of charity quickly turned into attempted robbery. Vladimir spun around. He knocked over two of the little beggars, grabbed the arm of a third and wrenched it out of his pockets. Just as he cocked his fist and prepared to give the children a stiff thrashing, they scattered. Vladimir looked down at his hand. Surely they weren't so afraid of him that they gave up and fled.

"Your mistake was handing the first boy a coin."

Vladimir turned and found himself staring straight into the eyes of a local constable. The man shook Vladimir's hand. Vladimir, in turn, hiccupped in the man's face.

"That's quite a noise you make," he said.

Vladimir nodded. "Is there any place in Kyakhta to spend the night? An inn perhaps? A lodge along the main street?" he said.

"You've come at the very worst time," the constable said. "This is the last weekend of trading before the entire town closes up shop. The Red Army is three days away. They've requested use of our facilities, even our homes. The kerfuffle you see here is the traders completing their final day of business before winter sets in."

"Why is the army coming? Is the war with Germany near?"

The constable rocked back and forth on his heels. "That I can't say."

"You can't say because you're not allowed? Or you can't say because you don't know?"

"I can't say."

Vladimir looked over the man's shoulder. In the distance the mountains surrounding Lake Baikal stood like an impenetrable barrier. He considered again the possibility of walking around the lake. Vladimir would most likely freeze to death or succumb to malnutrition if he tried.

"What about passage across the lake?" he said. "I need to get to Moscow. The railway in Irkutsk is my only hope."

The police officer reached into his jacket and produced a pocket watch. He gazed up at the sun peeking through the clouds and adjusted the timepiece, then placed it back in his pocket. He leaned in close to Vladimir's ear, so close that Vladimir's hiccups reverberated off his skin. "That kind of information comes with a price in this town."

Vladimir squinted. He reached inside his satchel and handed the man a fistful of rubles. The man looked down at the bills and then back up at Vladimir.

"That's all I have to spare," Vladimir said. "Any more and I won't have enough for my journey and any information you provide will be worthless."

The man tucked the money into his pocket. He pointed to a narrow two-story structure across the street. "In that green building, you'll find the best price for safe passage to Irkutsk. Ask for Yuran. He'll take care of you."

Vladimir turned and walked away from the unscrupulous official. He approached the green building and knocked on the door. Nearly a full minute passed before the door opened and a single bloodshot eyeball emerged. Vladimir looked over his shoulder at the police officer. Adjusting his pocket watch again, he motioned for Vladimir to say something.

"I'm looking for Yuran," Vladimir said.

The door opened farther and an old woman's face appeared. She stood a thumb's length shorter than the height of Vladimir's chest. The old woman's hair flowed down to her waist. Around her throat was a necklace made of animal bones. They might have been sheep toes or the broken portions of a yak's femur, for all Vladimir knew. Shrouded in black from head to foot, the woman gave Vladimir a peculiar look.

"Yuran is dead," she said.

Vladimir turned back and searched the street, but the policeman, if he even was an officer of the law, had disappeared. The streets still teemed with people. Their smell hovered in the air. Bartering voices hollered above the din, and lurking in the shadows of doorways were the vagrant children.

Vladimir turned back to the old woman. "I was told that Yuran could help me get over the mountains and across the lake."

"Where are you going?" she said. It was more of an accusation than a question.

"Moscow. I need to get to the railway in Irkutsk first. Can Yuran help me?"

"I already told you — he's dead. As dead as any dead man who ever died."

"Can you help me then?" he said.

The old woman peered at the crowd behind Vladimir. Two semi-feral steppe horses had just been spooked near the trading stations. One leapt onto its hind legs while the other galloped straight through the crowd.

"Step inside," she said and grabbed Vladimir's wrist. The old woman shut the door and now Vladimir was inside her darkened lair. The front room had the appearance of a nest, with tangles of sticks and dried leaves piled in the corners. Vladimir stood next to a life-size wooden carving of a Mongolian warrior. Draped atop the effigy was a collection of unwashed clothes. Dozens of clocks lined the walls, some hand-constructed out of oak, others ceramic, still others fashioned out of steel. Vladimir glanced down the single hallway leading to a sink and a washbasin. The hallway was lined with clocks as well, thirty at least, maybe more. He looked down at the old woman. She was staring at the wall like she'd forgotten he was even in the room.

Vladimir started to speak.

"Shhh," she said.

Vladimir looked at the wall as well. He hiccupped.

Three-point-seven seconds passed and then he hiccupped again. As the third hiccup sounded, the entire wall erupted in sound. All at once the clocks gave birth to their alarms. Birds flew out of trapdoors and tweeted. Bells chimed. Whistles squealed. In the far corner, a gong sounded. The sound was incredible — ten times louder than the clatter outside.

The old woman clasped her hands together and turned to Vladimir with a rapturous look on her face. "Isn't it wondrous?" she said.

"Does this happen every hour?"

The woman nodded, her red eyes wide and filled with amazement.

"Can you help me get across the lake?" he said.

"You will have to ask my son," she said.

"Yuran?"

"No. This is the third time I've made mention of it. Yuran died last month. He was kicked in the chest by a mule."

"That's terrible," Vladimir said.

The old woman wagged her finger in the air. "Never approach a mule from behind. It won't know your intentions," she said. "Now, as to crossing the mountains and the river, my son Dmitri will be able to help you." She took Vladimir by the arm and led him down the hallway. "Dmitri!" she yelled from beside the washbasin. "Dmitri! Come downstairs."

Vladimir heard the clumping of feet and an exhausted groan as the woman's son lumbered down the stairs. He was obese, with a thick head of hair and a protruding eyebrow, his forehead less than three centimeters in height. He gave Vladimir a confused look from the bottom of the stairs. "What?" he said.

"This young man with the hiccups. He needs to cross the Baikal River."

"It's a lake, not a river," her son said. "How many times do I need to tell you?"

"Then he needs to cross the lake. Can you take him tomorrow?"

The son looked at his wristwatch, even though at least forty wall clocks were in plain view. "Yes, I'll take him. There's a boat crossing in the afternoon. If we leave at five in the morning, we'll make it in plenty of time." He turned to go back upstairs.

"How much does it cost?" Vladimir said.

"Twelve rubles to me for the drive. Ten to the man on the boat," he said and shuffled upstairs.

"Then it's decided," the old woman said.

"I'm also seeking lodging for tonight," Vladimir said. "I have monies to pay."

"Excellent," the old woman said. "How much do you have to pay?"

Vladimir gave her a curious look. "How much does it cost?" he said.

The old woman's eyes shifted upward and to the left. Vladimir could see the gears shifting inside her head, her mind fluttering with the decision of how much to charge. She grinded her teeth together, looked back at Vladimir and shot out a number. "Forty rubles."

"I'll give you eight."

"Deal," the old woman said. "You can sleep in Yuran's old room. They removed his corpse just last week."

Vladimir crinkled his brow. "Didn't you say he died a month ago?" he said.

The old woman took Vladimir by the arm and led him up the stairs. "I've aired out the room in the time in between. After the mule kicked him, poor Yuran kept on for some four or five nights. I fed him berries and looked after him until he passed."

Together they walked down the hall to a small room where Vladimir was allowed to use the bedpan and the sink. He washed up with the old woman hovering outside the door and when he emerged, she led him to Yuran's room. She opened the door and let Vladimir in, then closed it quickly behind him. Vladimir heard the shifting of a lock on the other side. Then a second lock, this one from near the floorboards.

"Dmitri will gather you in the morning," she said through the door. "Have yourself a pleasant sleep."

Vladimir looked around. Despite the old woman's insistence, the room was windowless. There were no clocks on the walls either. A set of three light bulbs dangling from the ceiling was the only source of illumination. Atop the chest of drawers on the far wall, old pictures sat in frames. Vladimir set his satchel down and approached the pictures. They were all of children's play toys — a swing set in one, a teddy bear and ball left motionless on the side of the road in another. Nowhere in the photos was a child to be seen. No wide, innocent eyes or gap-toothed grins; just faded brown reminders of places where children had once found joy. Vladimir glanced under the bed for any sign of vermin, found none and sat down on the soft mattress. He reached inside his satchel, pulled out an apple and took a bite. When he did, the strangest sensation came over him. It was like he wasn't alone. A chill shot down his spine. Vladimir walked over and examined the cracks in the door. He turned around quickly, then paused. When he'd entered the green dwelling, it was nearing dusk. He would have eight hours, maybe as many as nine, to sleep before he and Dmitri were to leave.

Vladimir climbed into bed. He wrapped the musty-smelling

blankets over his chest and closed his eyes. The night did not go well. On the hour, every hour, the clocks (both upstairs and down) would detonate their long, fierce battle cries. Vladimir would just be drifting off to sleep, his mind heavy, his breathing in muted huffs, when the hour would strike and he would shoot out of bed. The first time the alarm sounded, Vladimir couldn't believe it. The next hour he was only mildly shocked. By the fourth and fifth occasions, he barely paid the noise any heed.

Vladimir was nestled quite comfortably in the dead man's pillow when something else entirely woke him from his sleep. He was in such a deep slumber that at first he thought it might have been the wind against his neck. This air was warm and it came in waves. Vladimir shifted, pulling himself from the depths of slumber, and suddenly, before even opening his eyes, he knew it was a person breathing against his neck. The mattress had sunk under weight greater than his own. Vladimir opened a single eyeball. The old woman was sitting on the bed, looming over top of him, her red eyes swirling, mouth bent into a twisted smile. In her hand was a branch covered in berries.

"Your friends are all dead," she said. "We're alone now, you and I. There's no one left in the whole world."

The ceiling lights quivered.

Her wrinkled hand rubbed his cheek.

"That's okay, Yuran. You'll be all right. Mother's here," she said. "Eat your berries like a good boy." She held the berries over Vladimir's mouth. His lips refused to part, and the look in the old woman's bloodshot eyes shifted from compassion to determination. Vladimir still hadn't moved when she shoved the berries hard against his mouth. The coarse branch scraped his chin and still he refused to open. Then, against his will, he hiccupped. His lips parted and two filthy morsels slipped in before he could close them.

Instantly the old woman's face changed. She shifted her hand from his cheek to his forehead. "Oh, my dear Yuran," she said. "I'll nurse you back to health."

Vladimir could feel the berries inside his mouth like two tiny, unbroken balloons. Up close this woman's eyes looked like they'd been pecked at by ravenous blackbirds. Her face contained a galaxy of pores, literally thousands of outlets for perspiration eclipsed only by a single round pimple on her cheek, a red sun orbited by a miniature white mole. The old woman stood up. Vladimir hiccupped again but he didn't expel the fruit.

Her voice was haunting. It skipped like a broken record player. "I'll check to see if you're still alive in the morning, my dear boy," she said. The old woman kissed him on the forehead, a long, wet fastening of her lips to his skin. When she pulled away, there was a clicking sound like a tongue ungluing from the top of one's mouth.

She left the room and locked it behind her. Vladimir glanced around the darkened corners of this small cell. He was alone again. He spat the berries out onto the floor and stood up out of bed. He wouldn't sleep anymore tonight.

The next day, in a village named Listvyanka on the other side of Lake Baikal, Vladimir placed a single foot inside the public transport bus that would take him to the city of Irkutsk. Before he could enter all the way, Dmitri wrapped his short arms around Vladimir's shoulders. Tears streamed down the large man's face. Over the past seven and a half hours, Dmitri had poured his heart out to Vladimir, first on the drive to the passage vessel that would take them across lake and later on the ship itself. Dmitri hadn't intended on traversing the lake with his new hiccupping friend, but once he discovered he'd found a sympathetic ear, it seemed he couldn't help himself. The scandal was too great. Too long had his shoulders been weighed down by a planet of regret. Dmitri told Vladimir everything. About the bad business dealings, his brother Yuran's refusal to own up to his obligations. About the illegitimate child begotten to a syphilis-ridden prostitute. How he'd arranged to spook the mule with a flash of gunpowder just as his brother stood behind it. Now he, Dmitri, the good son, the pious one — morally impervious in every way — was a murderer. His brother Yuran was dead. His mother was overcome with grief. The prostitute had complained to the local magistrate and insisted the child was his. Still his family owed a fortune to the government bank and, worse, even more to unscrupulous moneylenders. How would he escape this deep blue anguish that clung to him like a shadow?

Vladimir looked at the large man, who was red-faced and weeping, then stepped into the bus. He struggled for something — anything — to say, words that would assuage Dmitri's guilt and stop his descent into ruin. Nothing came to him, nothing poignant at least. "You will be okay, my friend," Vladimir said as the bus door closed between them. Off the bus went down the road. Vladimir took a single look back. Dmitri had fallen to his knees. He slumped forward, his hands dipped into the mud, and then the poor man, now purple in the face and sweating profusely, collapsed. Onlookers rushed to his aid. Vladimir couldn't quite believe it. All those months in the hospital, he'd never witnessed a heart attack. The bus was rounding a corner. No one aboard seemed to have noticed the large man's demise. Vladimir went to stand up, only to realize he had no resuscitation skills, no reason to think he'd be able to help. Already a crowd had formed around Dmitri. Vladimir put his head down. The other passengers had noticed his hiccups. One of them cleared his throat and waved his hand downward in an appeal to get Vladimir to cut it out. Vladimir slumped down in his seat. He wrapped his arms around his satchel, made himself as small as possible and leaned his head against the window. He hiccupped eleven times before finally falling asleep.

His dreams were unlike any he'd experienced before. Unconscious hallucinations inhabited his mind. Vladimir was a general in the army, standing at the edge of a bridge as the Germans advanced carrying torches, eyes blackened, marching in monotone rhythm to the sound of his hiccups. In the background, Mother Russia was ablaze. No amount of sleet or snow or rain could douse the two-meter-high flames. He alone as general was tasked with giving the order to blow up the bridge. The army would retreat to the north, back to Vladimir's home, where every memory was muted in silver dust. Vladimir raised his hand. The bridge exploded and collapsed, but the Germans — wearing the crimson uniforms of Mephistopheles — refused to halt their advance. Like Norwegian lemmings, they tumbled into the abyss, each step taken in time with Vladimir's internal pendulum.

The world had changed. Yet he knew nothing of the world that had existed before. Vladimir's sleepy village, the walls of the hospital, the jungles of Mongolia were all hiding places. He was reborn in the waterfall and now stood anew. Only the world was in flux; it was on fire, and Vladimir was an iceberg melting away, dripping, with the person he used to be licking at his liquefying carcass.

His dreams shifted and he was flying. Soldiers dropped liquid fire from planes. Vladimir's father flew the lead aircraft. He stared at his son from the cockpit of his bomber, a delirious, mesmerizing stare that Vladimir returned with confusion.

Vladimir fought against sleep. His conscious mind entered his dreams and tried to pull him out.

He was awoken by a sudden crash. The bus veered danger-ously to the right. Vladimir felt himself slip. His eyes opened just as he slid the length of his seat and fell straight to the floor. The passengers toppled like dominos, shrieking and screaming, their scrambling limbs entangled as the bus lurched to a stop, its entire right side firmly entrenched in a ditch. An elderly woman's shoe was pressed against Vladimir's face. He hoisted himself up. Vladimir stood akilter with the others as they moved single file out through the emergency door at the back of the bus and into the ditch, then to the side of the road. The driver checked on his passengers. There were fourteen in all, three wounded, none severely, the worst injury a suspected broken ankle of a middle-aged Estonian woman. He surveyed the damage to the vehicle next. The front axle had disengaged and one of the tires had been torn to shreds. The driver stood in the center of the road, looked both ways and then scratched his head.

"What we need is a telephone," he said to no one in par-ticular.

Vladimir approached. "How far is it to Irkutsk?"

"We're almost there," the man said. "Perhaps a thirty-minute drive away. Maybe less."

Vladimir looked down the road in the direction the vehicle had been traveling and then back at his fellow travelers pulling their suitcases from the wreck. The injured woman was testing her ankle against the ground while her husband held her up by the shoulder.

"Do you have a plan?" Vladimir said.

The man scratched his head again. His eyebrows gathered together like those of a genetically challenged primate. "Another bus will come by before nightfall. We'll have to wait and see if they have room."

"And if they don't?"

"Then I suppose we'll have to walk."

Vladimir looked down the road again. He hefted his satchel over his shoulder. "I'm going to walk ahead," he said to the group. "Does anyone want to come with me?"

The crowd in the road stared back at him, expressionless.

Vladimir shrugged his shoulders. "I'll send help if I find it," he said and started walking away from the wreckage. He hadn't made it twenty paces before the driver came running up to him. He put his arm around Vladimir's shoulder.

"There's a quicker way." The man pointed to the tall grass field with a walkway cut through its center a half kilometer down the road. "The road circles around and past two separate villages. But if you head directly through that field and stay on course due west, you'll reach your destination in a third of the time."

Vladimir cast him an apprehensive glare. He'd spent weeks walking through barren fields on his way out of Mongolia. Nothing on this journey home, it seemed, would be easy.

"You're sure of this?" he said.

The man nodded.

"If I stay on the road, perhaps I can send some help your way," Vladimir said.

"Who are you going to send?" the driver said. "I doubt there's a stray team of mechanics wandering the countryside. Even if you found one, we need a hoist to lift the bus out of the ditch. We're best off waiting here for the next bus to pick us up. You're best off waiting as well."

"I have to get home," Vladimir said.

The driver took a step back. Their eyes locked and then he turned and walked back to the group, who had already fashioned a makeshift circle out of their suitcases. A game of cards started up.

Vladimir marched down the road. A half kilometer later, when he came to the walkway through the tall grass, he took one last look back. The people on the road were indistinct; he couldn't have picked their faces out of a lineup if he'd tried. Vladimir looked back farther. Lake Baikal was hidden behind a series of hills. Beyond that was the township of Kyakhta with its crooked law enforcement, beggars and thieves, its murderous brothers and at least one infant stricken with a congenital disease affecting mucous membranes, the aorta and all manner of other important bones and organs. Gone was Usurpet and his lascivious brood. Also Gog and the waterfall, the lands in which Vladimir used to hunt.

Vladimir stepped into the path and left his past behind.

eleven

Night had long settled into the marbled sky when Vladimir arrived on the outskirts of the city. He crossed through yet another field, the eighteenth he'd traversed in the past two hours. Just an hour ago he waved to a farmer herding goats. Then dark fell. Vladimir kept his eyes glued to his compass. He never veered from the direction of due west.

Slowly the city of Irkutsk appeared to him as a warm orange glow in the distance. Vladimir smiled. Soon he would be sitting inside a railway car, drinking tea with lemon and eating some kind of pastry — something fancy with cinnamon baked right into the bread and layers of white sugar on top. He smacked his lips and ran to the edge of a small cliff. Vladimir stood at the top and looked at Irkutsk in all its glory. It wasn't Moscow by any stretch of the imagination. But it was civilization — teeming, brilliant civilization with lights and theater houses, women and girls, life and vitality.

Vladimir leapt over the edge and glided along one foot to the bottom, smiling all the while from ear to ear. He stepped out from behind a chaparral of prickly bushes and stopped dead in his tracks. There in front of him was a man sitting in a small cage on the back of a green pickup truck. The truck, in turn, was hidden behind a collection of tall pine trees. The cage was barely a meter tall and the man's face was bruised and beaten, his one eye swollen to the extent of closure. His clothing was covered in dried blood and soot. He flashed Vladimir a desperate look.

"Help me," he whispered.

Vladimir looked left and then right; he looked back up the incline he'd just descended.

"Help me," the man said again. "I'm a soldier. I've been taken captive."

Vladimir leaned in close. He hiccupped in the man's face.

The soldier's eyes grew wide like he was about to launch into cardiac arrest. "Shhh!" he whispered. "You'll wake them up."

"Who?" Vladimir said.

The man gestured toward the front of the vehicle.

Vladimir peered to his left without moving his feet. "What kind of soldier are you?" he said.

"I'm an airman in the Red Army." The man pointed to the blue insignia on his shoulder.

"Is that the Russian or German army?"

"Russian!" he said in a hard whisper. "Now get me out of here."

Vladimir angled his body to the left again. He took a single cautious step toward the front of the car. There were indeed two men sitting in the front. Across their laps were large guns, weapons the likes of which Vladimir had never seen. He stepped back and leaned in close to talk to the man. "Are they Germans?"

"They're Japanese!" he said. "Look at their skin and their eyes."

Vladimir glanced back again. Their skin was a light brown color. Their eyes were distinctly foreign as well. "So they're kamikazes."

"No, you idiot. They're soldiers, not pilots."

"I fail to see the difference," Vladimir said.

"They're Japanese soldiers. That's all you need to know."

"Whatever their nationality," Vladimir said, "they have guns. If I try to free you, they'll shoot me dead. I was just shot at the other day by an enraged farmer. It was not a pleasant experience. I don't want to be shot at again."

The Russian soldier grabbed Vladimir by the collar. He pulled him in close. "You listen to me, you *oslayob*! If you don't get me out of here, those men will torture me and burn me alive. Then they'll do the same to any other Russian — soldier or civilian — they might meet. Their army left them behind to do one thing — kill poor bastards like me. And if you don't stop hiccupping, if you don't get the keys and let me out of here, I'll never see my son again. I'll never see my wife. I'll end up dead on the side of the road and so will a hundred other Russians before they're through with us."

Vladimir didn't blink. He didn't even move as the man breathed against his nose. For the first time since the Waterfall of Ion, he fashioned that familiar vacuous stare.

The soldier looked deep into Vladimir's eyes. "Help me," he said again.

"Release me," Vladimir said slowly.

The man increased his grip.

Vladimir didn't move. He didn't try to remove the man's hands. He just stared straight ahead, waiting, hiccupping, his brown eyes resolute. Eventually the soldier's hands softened. He loosened his grip on Vladimir's collar and then released him altogether. Vladimir took two steps back. He looked around. The truck was shielded by the trees, with no chance a random passerby would stumble upon them. Night had fully overtaken the day. From where he stood, Vladimir could no longer see the bright lights of Irkutsk. Above, the moon hung like a broken coin in the sky.

"Where are the keys?" Vladimir said.

The soldier edged to the front of his cage and pointed into the car. "In the ignition," he said.

Vladimir stepped softly and looked inside. He could see the keys inside the ignition, resting against the driver's long black gun.

"Reach inside and get them," the soldier said.

"The door's locked," Vladimir whispered.

The soldier scrambled inside his cage. He motioned Vladimir over to the passenger's side. "It's unlocked over here," he said.

Vladimir cast him a dubious look.

The soldier flashed back his pleading eyes.

Following a moment's hesitation, Vladimir set his satchel on the ground. As delicately as possible, he placed his hand on the door handle and pressed his fingers down. The door pried open. Vladimir pulled it toward him carefully, a few centimeters at a time. The resulting creak was so loud it sent shockwaves through Vladimir's heart. He turned and glared at his fellow Russian. The soldier nodded eagerly and motioned for Vladimir to continue. Vladimir pulled the door even more ajar until his torso fit through and then he leaned inside the car. He could smell the enemy soldiers, feel their breath against his cheek. Vladimir stood on his toes and grasped the keys in his hand. Gently, he pulled them out of the ignition and backed out the way he'd come. As he exited the car, Vladimir hiccupped once, loudly and with his mouth open. The blood froze in his veins. He shut his mouth and shifted his eyes. The driver shuffled in his seat, exhaled a snore in stages out through his nose and then turned his head to the side and went back to sleep. He never even opened his eyes.

Vladimir exhaled a long, deep breath.

He walked around to the back of the pickup and handed the keys to the soldier. Madly, and making more noise than Vladimir could have imagined possible, the soldier flipped through the keys until he spotted one that might fit the lock on the cage. He inserted the key and the cage door flew open. The soldier climbed out, landed softly on his feet and brushed past Vladimir. He walked around to the passenger's side, opened the door and grabbed the gun from the enemy soldier's lap. The man inside sat up in a start but it was too late. Without hesitation, the soldier fired two quick bursts with the machine gun. The dying man screamed. A third and fourth round of gunfire sounded. In aimless streaks of crimson, the driver's blood splattered all over the back window. Then the gunfire ceased. Suddenly Vladimir felt an unparalleled intensification of all his senses. Every minute aperture on his face distended fully. His eyelids opened and closed like the batting of two enormous fans. A dense layer of sound blanketed the trees — the echo of the gunfire reverberating against the hill; the Russian soldier's guttural scream; the last gasps of air from the Japanese. The world slowed down and all that Vladimir could hear, all he could see and taste and feel, was death.

The soldier turned and pointed the gun at Vladimir, his eyes filled with bloodlust.

Instantly Vladimir realized how rash and stupid he'd been. Since the moment they'd met, he'd made no real allegiance with this man. He had found a prisoner locked in a cage, was tricked into believing the prisoner was a military man and then fell victim to a perennial tale of woe involving a bright-eyed young son and a soon-to-be-widowed bride. He'd risked his life for the sole purpose of handing the prisoner a gun. Vladimir cursed himself. The urge to run manifested in his chest and then was quickly dismissed. Taking flight would be undignified. He would stand his ground and meet his fate like a man.

"Do you want a turn?" the soldier said.

"What do you mean?"

He took his hand off the trigger and presented the gun to Vladimir. "Do you want to shoot them?"

A wave of relief flowed over Vladimir. "They're already dead, right?" he said.

The soldier looked inside the car. "Yes. They're dead."

"Then it probably doesn't make much sense for me to shoot them again."

The soldier shrugged his shoulders. He reached inside and grabbed a canister of water from the front seat. With one hand he opened it and took three long swigs. He held it in the air for Vladimir.

"No, thank you," Vladimir said.

The soldier pulled the dead man from the passenger seat and dragged his body away from the car. Then he went around to the other side and pulled out the driver. He lined their bodies up side by side and then searched inside the car for something. A minute passed before he found a long rectangular wallet and produced a picture. "My wife and my son," he said.

Vladimir nodded. It hadn't all been a lie.

When the soldier finished fishing around inside the truck, he set the gun down on the flatbed and reached out to shake Vladimir's hand. "You've done your country a great service today. Mother Russia is proud to have you as her son."

Vladimir took the man's hand in his. It was cold and trembled slightly.

"If there's anything I can do for you," he said, "anything at all, don't hesitate to ask."

"There is one thing," Vladimir said.

"What is it?"

"I have no papers. No documentation or anything to prove my identification."

"Were they stolen?" he said.

"Something like that," Vladimir said. "I believe I'll need some kind of identification to travel on the railway to Moscow."

"Wait one second," the soldier said. He reached inside the car and flipped through a stack of papers until he found what he was looking for. The man handed Vladimir a little booklet with three sheets of paper jutting out. "For travel purposes, your name is now officially Yevgeni Kaminski," he said. "Soldier in the Russian army. Twenty-three years of age."

Vladimir took the papers in his hand. "What happened to the real Yevgeni Kaminski?" he said.

The soldier pointed at the dead men on the ground. Their bloody corpses lay eerily still. Vladimir could hardly believe that just minutes ago they were people, men with families and hopes and fears and dreams. Now they littered the earth surrounding the trees.

"The Japanese must have killed him. They kept a pile of soldiers' papers in the car. There must be thirty or forty of these in here." He walked around to the front of the car and stepped into the driver's seat. "Can I drive you into Irkutsk?" he said.

Vladimir looked at the dark red blood splattered across the windows. A machine gun was sitting in the passenger's seat, another in the back of the truck.

"Thank you," he said. "But no. I'm going to walk."

The soldier reached out the window and shook Vladimir's hand again. "I'm forever in your debt," he said and fired up the engine.

The truck pulled out from behind the trees and onto a nearby road. Vladimir watched it drive away. He stood alone in the faint moonlight. Near him the dead bodies of the two Japanese soldiers lay motionless. Vladimir's hand was covered in tiny speckles of blood.

The next morning he presented the Russian soldier's papers at the Trans-Siberian railway station and climbed aboard a train heading toward Moscow. Sergei and Alexander, his doctors, awaited him.

twelve

Vladimir arrived in Moscow just as night settled in. Rather than procure accommodation, he wandered the cold streets alone and kept as far away from passersby as possible. He walked the Garden Ring, the circular avenue that wraps like a rubber band around the center of Moscow, several times until he grew tired and took refuge in a secluded spot behind the Imperial Bolshoi Theatre. The theater was a marvel to behold, a fusion of traditional Russian architecture with Ukrainian baroque elements imported from Central Europe. Built in 1824 after the ancient Petrovka Theatre had been brought down by fire, the Bolshoi Theatre had housed ballet and opera for over a century. Tonight the theater was premiering Boris Asafyev's musical reworking of *The Storm*, a play by Alexander Ostrovsky — a hulking ogre of a man, cruel but funny, and dead in 1886 of acute cardiac arrest. The crowd entering through the front doors was a mixture of theater critics, the genuinely curious, and traditional opera fans come to sneer in derision at Asafyev's modernist drama. Vladimir ignored the crowd and dozed off gently against the theater's back wall.

Vladimir awoke the next morning at dawn to the repetitive clank of a sledgehammer. He stood up, observed the deluge of snow that had fallen while he slept and then peered through an open window. Six workers, maybe as many as eight, were removing bricks from a wall inside. Behind them were two soldiers with guns slung over their shoulders. An old woman carrying a parcel full of books was passing by, staying close to the theater wall to avoid the fresh accumulation of snow.

Vladimir tapped her on the shoulder. "What are they doing?" he said.

The woman brought her eyebrows together and cast him a curious look. "What?" she hollered.

Vladimir repeated his query.

"I'm quite hard of hearing," the woman said. "You'll have to speak loudly."

Vladimir pointed inside the open window. "What are they doing?" he said.

The gray-haired lady shuddered a weary sigh; weary for the morning's chill, weary for this dotard and his relentless look of confusion, weary for the new world in which the elderly were forced to sell their parents' books — family heirlooms every one of them — to pay for bread and poultry. She stood up on her toes to peer inside. "Hold my bag and I'll go ask," she said. The old woman shoved her parcel into Vladimir's hands and, before he could stop her, she walked through an open doorway and right up to the soldiers. Vladimir ducked behind the wall while the old woman was inside. A minute passed before she returned.

"They're looking for Yakov's treasure," she said, largely satisfied with herself.

"Who's Yakov?" Vladimir said.

"You are an uneducated one, aren't you?"

"Well, do you know who he is?" Vladimir said, and before he knew it, she was shuffling off through the doorway to talk to the soldiers again. Vladimir ducked down a second time, wary of drawing unwanted attention. Two minutes later the old woman returned.

"Yakov is Yakov Bruce," she said. "Apparently he's been in all the news sheets recently. Yakov was an alchemist who practiced black magic back in the 1700s. The soldiers are searching for his books now. They say his books contain maps to locate treasures buried around Russia."

"Is that true?" Vladimir said.

"I'm not sure. I can go ask if you like," she said.

Vladimir put his hand on her shoulder. "No. That will be all right," he said.

The old woman looked down at her parcel full of volumes bequeathed to her by birthright, those she would be forced to sell that morning to feed her starving family. "Now do an old lady a kindness and help me carry these. It won't be but a few blocks."

Vladimir threw his bag over his shoulder and took one last look back at the theater. Here was Russia's present, chiseling away at its past. And beside it was Vladimir, nescient to both, so long had he been away. Vladimir had missed much. If a dozen revolutions had come and gone, he hadn't been informed. He assisted the elderly woman a total of seven city blocks — considerably more than she'd specified — before parting company with her outside of a shop specializing in antiques. He watched her storm inside and immediately begin berating the man at the front desk about the value and importance of her family's books. "Here I have a seminal work by Maximilian Voloshin!" she declared. "This volume contains the banned verses of Osip Mandelstam!"

The door slammed shut and Vladimir continued west in the direction of the hospital.

He stopped in the ankle-deep slush outside the hospital

gates. When last he had passed through these rusted metal doors, he'd been stolen away in the middle of the night, a dense sleep precluding him from knowing he had even left. Returning on this winter's day, he was no longer that troubled young boy Alexander had been forced to deliver to Gog. For the first time that he could remember, Vladimir was excited. He was excited about starting his new life, excited to see Sergei and Alexander again. Vladimir walked through the light snowfall with a smile across his face, entered the hospital's front doors and marched up the stairs to the fifth floor, where the doctors' offices were located. Sergei's office was first. Vladimir stopped outside the door and checked his reflection in a shiny brass plaque on the wall. He bared his teeth in front of the memorial. He rubbed his finger across his incisors to ensure they were clean. He checked his breath for odor, straightened his jacket, removed his hat to reveal his newly shorn hair and knocked on the office door.

A short, bald man with a walrus mustache and a hunch about his shoulders answered.

"Where's Dr. Namestikov?" Vladimir said.

The man had just taken a bite out of a creamy pastry and almost choked when he heard the first hiccup emerge from Vladimir's mouth.

"How long have you been hiccupping?" the man said.

"Twelve years."

The man dropped his *vatrushka* and gave Vladimir a stunned look. He poked his head out into the hallway, shifted his eyes side to side and then retreated into the office. At the last moment he whispered in a hushed voice, "If anyone asks, I never saw you." The man slammed the door shut and fastened the lock on the other side.

Puzzled, Vladimir headed down the hallway to find

Alexander. He arrived at the location of the doctor's office to discover the door missing. A stack of brown boxes was piled chest-high inside. Vladimir peered past them to find even more boxes and, beyond that, a few shelves covered in a thin but discernable layer of dust. He examined the door frame for Doctor Afiniganov's name or any indication to prove Alexander had once taken residence here. There was none. Vladimir began to doubt his memory. He'd only ever been up to these offices twice before, both times to see Sergei. This might not even be the right floor.

Vladimir walked down the stairs in the direction of the administration office. He remembered every twist and turn of the hallways, every stain in the ceiling and missing chip of paint on the walls. The sides of the hallway were still covered in the crash marks of gurneys and strange, unexplained blotches of discoloration from long ago. Vladimir turned down a second hallway. Along the way he passed two patients and a nurse, each of whom cast him an inquisitive gaze. Whereas years ago the looks of others were characterized primarily by curiosity, sometimes even sympathy, these stares were layered with suspicion.

Something had changed.

Something was different here.

Vladimir approached the administration desk. Three large green chairs sat unoccupied behind the counter. He rang a small bell atop a stack of papers. The instant the bell rang, one of the chairs moved. Vladimir leaned forward. The middle chair was occupied by a slight woman with a mouse's face, her torso hidden in an oversize olive-colored blanket. She'd been fast asleep when he arrived and only after a half minute of Vladimir's repetitive yelping did she finally stir and begin to clear thick chunks of debris from her eyes.

A rustling of feet sounded from across the hall and a

second woman came to the desk. This one was large, wide-eyed and fully awake. "Sir, how long have you been hiccupping?" the large woman said. "Sir, I'm asking you a question." The mouse-like woman jumped to her feet. "He's not hiccupping. He's just pretending to hiccup to get a rise out of you. Isn't that right?" She flashed Vladimir a subtle glare that told him to go along with her.

Vladimir nodded and held his breath to keep the yelps in. The small woman walked around the counter and grabbed Vladimir by the elbow. "I'm going to take this funny man here out for a walk. I'll be back soon." She pulled strongly on Vladimir's arm. Unsure quite what to do, Vladimir followed her lead and allowed the woman to drag him all the way outside through the exterior doors. Once out in the snow, the woman let go of his arm and took a long look at him.

"Vladimir?" she said. "Is it really you?"

"How do you know my name?"

"It's Ilvana. Ilvana Strekov. I'm a nurse's aide here at the hospital. I traveled with you and Doctor Afiniganov to Mongolia."

A sudden recollection triggered in Vladimir's brain. The coach ride up and down the valley. The hulking Siberian oaf who carried him through the marsh. That messy puddle of drool he left in that frail woman's lap. Vladimir squinted and looked closely. He remembered a nurse trailing along toward the back of their procession as they approached Gog's residence. But he couldn't quite recall her features. Ten years had passed. Would this Ilvana have looked the same back then? Would she have had the same hardened wrinkles about her eyes, the same quill of white hair set in a bun atop her head?

"How do you know it's me?" he said.

"Well, you've grown into a young man — a handsome one, I might add." She looked into his wide brown eyes and then down to his strong jaw and high cheekbones. "I would recognize your eyes anywhere," she said. "Plus, there's . . ."

"The hiccupping . . ."

"Yes, the hiccupping. My God, Vladimir, have you been hiccupping all this time?"

"I have," he said. "But it doesn't affect me anymore. I hardly notice it. I found peace standing in the Waterfall of Ion . . ." Vladimir was about to launch into a long, detailed account of the last ten years of his life when Ilvana Strekov grabbed him by the arm again and led him farther away from the building.

She shot a nervous glance at the hospital walls and whispered, "You can't be here. It's not safe. You don't know what they'll do if they find you."

"But I came to see Doctor Namestikov and Doctor Afiniganov. I want to thank them for everything they did for me."

As Vladimir spoke, Ilvana's eyelids started to droop. She faltered a little on her feet. Before her eyes closed fully, Vladimir touched her on the shoulder.

"Doctor Afiniganov is dead!" Ilvana shouted, startling herself awake. She moved in close. "Alexander died a year and a half ago."

"What about Doctor Namestikov?"

"He's here."

"Then may I see him?"

"It's not that easy."

"Is this about the war? About the Germans?"

She shook her head. "It has nothing to do with that."

"Please, I must see him. He was like a father to me. I can wait if his schedule's full."

Ilvana stole another wary glance back at the building and

then whispered in Vladimir's ear. "I will arrange for you to see him. Return here, to this very spot, at midnight tonight. I'll be waiting by the doors. I promise to do everything in my power to ensure that you speak with Doctor Namestikov in person. He can explain the rest to you. But you must swear to me that you won't speak to a single living soul until that time — not at the hospital or in a restaurant or even on the street. You must stay out of sight and most definitely out of earshot. Do you understand?"

Vladimir nodded.

"Good. Then I will see you tonight."

With those words, Ilvana Strekov stole her way back into the building, leaving Vladimir to stand outside in the cold and the snow.

That evening he would return to discover the shock of his life.

thirteen

Fourteen hours after he had left the premises, Vladimir found himself back in the exact same spot where Ilvana had left him. Hiccupping and hungry, he waited in the snow, an utterly conspicuous figure standing alone with a shoulder bag containing all of his worldly possessions. Forty minutes passed and Vladimir was starting to believe that Ilvana would never arrive. Finally, he heard a loud thump from the other side of the door where the nurse's aide was to emerge. He waited for some kind of signal for him to approach — a second thump, the rap of knuckles against aluminum, Ilvana's voice maybe. When a full minute passed and still Vladimir had heard nothing, he approached the entranceway.

The door was slightly ajar. Vladimir pulled on the handle and out flopped the unconscious body of Ilvana Strekov. The poor thing had fallen asleep against the inside of the doorway, her hand still attached to the key in the door handle. Vladimir tapped her gently on the cheek. When she didn't respond, he shook her, softly at first and then vigorously, until she woke up.

"What happened?" Ilvana said.

"You tell me."

Ilvana stood up. She wiped the snow off of her elbow. "I must have dozed off," she said. "The doctor is waiting for you."

With deliberate stealth, Ilvana — now fully awake — hurried Vladimir through a series of corridors and stairwells. After her brief respite against the doorway, she appeared to be an entirely different person. Determined. Knowledgeable about the path the two of them should follow. They exited the main building and hurried across a shadowy courtyard before entering a second building using a set of keys the nurse's aide kept in her uniform pocket.

The moment they walked through this door, Vladimir was overwhelmed by a flush of thick, gloomy air. In a single breath, he inhaled a blood-splatter collage of torment, fear and lunacy. His stomach retched. Vladimir felt light-headed. His knees wobbled slightly. Ilvana grabbed his elbow and ushered Vladimir up a flight of stairs and down another corridor, this one resembling the aftermath of a battle scene, gross with the stench of urine and filled with agonized screams originating from closed doors on either side. Two passed-out bodies littered the hallway. Ilvana stopped at an apparently random door. With the terror of this place building around her, she fumbled before inserting the key in the hole. Finally she pulled Vladimir inside and closed the door.

They'd entered a small room consisting of two chairs, a single table and a flickering light bulb dangling precariously from a frayed wire overhead. The barren walls contained no window. The room was like a prison cell with white walls instead of bars. Ilvana motioned for Vladimir to sit in one of the chairs and then hurried off through a door at the end of the room. In her haste, she left the door ajar. Vladimir could hear her speaking with someone down the hall. After a few seconds, the voices stopped. Vladimir was waiting in his chair when the most curious noise emerged from beyond the doorway. Someone was hiccupping.

The hiccups sounded all wrong to Vladimir. The volume of each yelp varied from convulsion to convulsion. Moreover, the interval between each hiccup was inconsistent. Vladimir could have set a metronome by the sound of his. Every 3.7 seconds, another hiccup was destined to shoot forth from his mouth. This sound echoing down the hallway was regular, there was no doubt. But upon close inspection, miniscule discrepancies in their duration and spacing revealed that these hiccups lacked the steadiness of Vladimir's own. There was something else they lacked, something entirely crucial that a casual observer might not notice but that Vladimir found patently obvious — urgency. These hiccups lacked the pressing, critical need to escape the dark cell from which they came.

A series of hushed whispers sounded. They were growing closer. Then a single set of footsteps clambered down the hall, accompanied strangely by the jangle of chains. A face appeared in the doorway. It was one Vladimir would have known anywhere. But it had changed forever.

fourteen

Sergei Namestikov stood in the doorway, a shadow of the man he once was. His wrists and ankles were bound by chains. His once-proud mane of dark hair had all but disappeared, replaced by a circular bald patch atop his head and long, shaggy gray locks flowing down the back of his neck. Whereas once his face had maintained a close, clean shave, a beard had taken root at the tip of his chin, spurting forward in wild chunks of gray and white. He was wearing a bright blue hospital gown, the kind the patients wore in the psychiatric unit. It clung to his chest, where his bones formed a stepladder up to his neck. Down below, the gown was cut short at the thighs to reveal his bony white knees. Sergei had lost so much weight. Every few seconds, a hiccup emerged from his mouth.

Sergei raised his chained hands in exhilaration. "Vladdy, my boy! Is it really you?"

Vladimir was almost too stunned to speak. "Yes," he said.

"Oh, how long I've waited to see your face again. I always knew you'd return."

Sergei's eyes shifted.

He leaned in close.

"You haven't come here to kill me, have you?"

"No," Vladimir said.

"Because they're sending someone to kill me — that's the rumor anyways."

"Please," Vladimir said, "you must tell me what happened. Why are you in here? Why are you hiccupping? Did I give you the hiccups?"

Sergei let out a wild laugh. "Of course not, my boy. You can't catch the hiccups from someone." His laughter descended from uncontrolled hilarity into a slight, humorless gurgle and then disappeared altogether. For the first time since he entered the room, Sergei seemed to notice that Vladimir was still hiccupping. A sadness filled his expression. "So no one was able to cure you after all, were they?"

Vladimir took a seat at the table. He beckoned Sergei to join him. With great caution, the doctor sat down across from Vladimir.

"I found peace in my soul in the Waterfall of Ion . . ." Vladimir launched into a long, detailed account of the past ten years. From the carriage ride delivering him into the valley at the base of the great Burkhan Khaldun mountain, to the death of Tomchar under the waterfall, to Gog's silence and the path he forced Vladimir to walk every day, to the year he spent in the wild, culminating in his forced entry into the Waterfall of Ion — Vladimir lay the last decade bare before Sergei.

The doctor listened intently. When it was all done, Sergei's eyes turned red. He slammed his fist on the table. "That blasted Alexander!" Sergei hit the hard metal surface three times until Vladimir was forced to reach out and take his hand. Sergei leaned forward, their hands still linked, and whispered in Vladimir's ear. "I know I can trust you," he said between hiccups. "You were like a son to me. You would never hurt me. You would never take their side, would you?"

"Never," Vladimir said. "You helped me when I was a little boy. I'll never forget that. I would do anything for you."

"Good," Sergei said. He let go of Vladimir's hand. Sergei looked back down the hallway to ensure they were alone. He glanced under the table and shifted his eyes around the room. Finally satisfied, he looked Vladimir square in the eye. Sergei stopped hiccupping. Just like that. In a single instant, his hiccups disappeared, leaving Vladimir's convulsive yelps to fill the air alone.

Vladimir's eyes grew wide. "How did you do that?"

Sergei rubbed the long gray whiskers on his gaunt face. "I've been faking them this whole time."

"For how long?"

"For eighteen months now — a full year and a half," Sergei said.

Vladimir couldn't tell whether Sergei was proud of his accomplishment or heartbroken that it had come this far. "Why would you do that?" he said.

"Because of Alexander, that cad!" Sergei exclaimed. He slammed his fist again in anger.

Vladimir cast a brief glance at the open doorway. Ilvana still hadn't come back. "Please," he said. "Explain everything to me. Start at the beginning."

Sergei rubbed his eyes. They seemed to have aged a hundred years since Vladimir last saw them, their esteemed influence fading and leaving an unhinged turmoil in its place. Sergei heaved as though he might begin to convulse. He scraped his fingers along the sides of his face. "I will start, as you suggest, at the beginning," he said.

★ ★ ★

"In the evening hours before Alexander stole you away from the hospital," Sergei said, "I suffered both my greatest indignity and what would amount to the greatest triumph of my entire life. I caught Alexander in the arms of my wife. Technically she was my ex-wife, but that is no matter. She was my wife. We exchanged vows before a priest in a garden under cherry trees. She promised to love me until death do us part, in sickness and in health, in front of two hundred witnesses. My grandmother was there. Members of congress were invited. Several attended. What matter is it that years later we signed a piece of paper stating the marriage was null and void? We took vows in the name of Christ! And then to find her in Alexander's arms, to have her kiss his lips and dangle off him as though she were some new appendage he'd grown out of his kidney — what heights of humiliation was I expected to accept? What manner of man would I be if I stood by impotent and weepy-eyed as they cavorted shamelessly in front of me?

"I picked up a swirling mass of red, pink and purple wine and I dashed it upon her. Oh, Vladimir, I can't tell you what exhilaration it is to strip someone of their dignity after they've deliberately stolen yours." For a single moment Sergei's eyes recaptured a little of their old shine. "I was dragged from that place and tossed in the street like a dog. Two thugs roughed me up in an alley. They left me to crawl to my car, bleeding and battered, with bruises all over my face. But I didn't care. They could have killed me then and there and I would have died happy.

"That evening I returned home and the first thing I did was give my maid Tatiana a stiff pounding from behind. Oh, don't look at me like that. The poor dear had pined for me for months. I had at her like an untamed beast and then collapsed in my bed, covered in sweat, blood and semen. Covered in life! As I penetrated my maid's large, supple entry, never could

I have imagined that at that very moment, Alexander and his cronies were stealing you away. How appropriate it was for Alexander to do his dirty work in the basest of all hours, where criminals and drug addicts roam free and the meek and incredulous rule the dark of night.

"When I arrived at the hospital the next day, my first action was to go to your bedside. I'd hardly slept, so great was my worry. I knew after that afternoon at Markus's office, there was something deep inside that you couldn't control. A darkness had crept into the innermost reaches of your soul. I had to find you, to speak to you, to reason with you, to care for you not as a physician, but as a father would. You weren't in your bed. I stormed through the hospital floor you'd called home for two years, searched every room, peered in every deserted crook and cranny. I summoned all available members of the staff and we divided into groups. When our search of the hospital revealed nothing, we stretched out into the streets. I had orderlies, nurses and police officers — every able body I could find — searching for you. It was no use. You were gone.

"Only as the day became night did I realize that Alexander was also nowhere to be found. You were missing and Alexander had taken an unexplained leave of absence for three weeks' time. This was no coincidence. I knew immediately what he'd done. I called an emergency meeting of the hospital's senior staff. They had to be made aware of Alexander's treason. Before these men, I gave an impassioned speech quoting both Bakunin and Chaadayev and thoroughly depicting the empirical evidence at hand. You can imagine the ache in my heart when my presentation fell on deaf ears. No one would believe me. Word of the incident at the ballroom had spread and my impeccable reputation was now entirely suspect. The hospital board members insisted that I stay home from work until I abandoned my obsession with Alexander's misdeeds.

"For weeks I languished in bed. The agony of it all was too much to bear. Alexander had robbed me of my wife, Asenka, and now he had stolen my son — perhaps not by blood, but in the innermost reaches of my heart, you were my child, Vladimir.

"When Alexander returned from his mysterious absence, I accosted him outside the hospital gates. Would you believe that he denied everything? He looked me straight in the eye and proclaimed he didn't have the foggiest notion of what had become of you. He conjured up an absurd story about having attended a conference in Yekaterinburg all this time. That duplicitous charlatan! I had it in my mind to do away with him right then and there with my bare hands. And I would have too if reason hadn't intervened. You see, as strong as I was in my better days, I knew deep inside that no matter how badly I wanted to tear him from limb to limb, it would've been exceedingly difficult for me to defeat Alexander in an evenhanded bout of fisticuffs. Instead, I returned to the hospital and lodged formal charges. I burst through the office of the police and told them to arrest Alexander Afiniganov for kidnapping. I took my complaints as far as the Kremlin.

"No one would believe me! They thought that I was in the wrong, that I was the evildoer! The incident at the Isirk Ballroom preceded me. My good name had been ruined.

"You see, Vladimir, it is my curse that I alone could perceive the iniquitous black fog of hypocrisy that coiled behind Alexander as he walked, the way it merged with dark corners in unlit rooms and interfered with the illumination of anything daring to resemble the truth. This curse destroyed me. The hospital grew tired of my constant accusations and fired me outright. Days after my medical career crumbled to dust, I learned that my maid was with child. She refused any suggestion to terminate the pregnancy and insisted on seeing the birth all the way through. Those four and a half minutes of pleasure — no not pleasure: the exorcism of my rage in which I thrashed Tatiana against the washbasin in her room — they were my undoing as much as anything that happened at the ballroom. I waited the full nine months until the baby was born, praying all the while for it to somehow look like my elderly driver Afin. No such miracle occurred. When this bastard child emerged, it was like looking into a mirror. The boy was mine. With great reluctance, after months of enduring Tatiana's pleas, I made an honest woman of her. We married in a simple civil ceremony on a Wednesday afternoon.

"Vladimir, I can't begin to understand the pain you've experienced. And nothing I've gone through could possibly compare. But can you imagine for just one moment what it's like to have loved someone as deeply as I loved Asenka, to have achieved a profound, intimate connection on all levels — emotional, spiritual, sexual — only to have your partner's love turn sour and ferment like a nasty boil left to fester in the sun? And then to be forced to spend your married days with some simple-minded imbecile who loves you unconditionally no matter how vicious you are? It is an unbearable truth in life that love thrives on stillness. What we are made to endure in the here and now is damned by the fading color of the past."

Sergei had begun his diatribe with conviction, but with each word his bravado faded into hollow pathos. Sergei's voice — once strong and assertive — now flowed in waves; it soared to a crescendo, crashed and doubled over before fading like the tides. Unexpectedly, ferociously, it would rise again.

"Tatiana nursed the baby into a small child as my riches

faded. For years my status at the hospital had protected me from the ills of Stalin's economic upheaval. After my dismissal, I was no longer immune. What's more, my outward display of indignation at the Kremlin caused my name to be placed on a list. Before dawn on a Tuesday morning in early spring, government agents stormed into my home. At gunpoint, they took possession of the house my father had left me. I was given a paltry sum and forced to move into a small apartment overlooking a meat-packing plant. Tatiana and our son came along, of course. To my great surprise, so did Tatiana's mother, a deaf elderly Ukrainian woman with an odorous foot fungus and two cats who trailed her every move. She lived in the walk-in closet in our apartment, cooked her meals on the radiator, and whenever one of her cats misbehaved, she would throw it off the balcony and then have the audacity to insist that I purchase a new one when the creature failed to survive the fall.

"Looking back with the keen eye of hindsight, my fall from grace began when Alexander won that prestigious golden plaque for finishing first in our class at Tomsk University. If I'd somehow bested him, if I'd managed in some way to eclipse his scholastic supremacy and miraculously won that plaque, my life would have turned out quite differently. I would have been the more revered doctor. I would have been invited to the Isirk Ballroom that night and had the pleasure of watching Alexander carried out by his boots. He would be sitting here in this damned asylum, not me!" Sergei waved his chained hands absently in the air. "But I never won that plaque. It never sat on the wall in my study. Life was simply that cruel."

He cleared his throat and looked expectantly at Vladimir.

Vladimir stared in wonder at his doctor. "But you didn't

tell me how you came to be in this place," Vladimir said. "Why have you been faking the hiccups? What became of Alexander?"

Sergei's eyes turned a slight shade of yellow.

"I haven't even told you the most outrageous part of all. Years after he stole you away, Alexander actually had the audacity to publish a paper on your condition. That insolent *zadnitsa* linked the symptom of incurable hiccups to the disease of mental illness. I knew this wasn't true. At least, I knew there was no way for him to verify that your hiccups and the malaise in your mind were inextricably linked. I rallied against his findings; I did everything in my power to discredit them. There was a flaw, you see, in Alexander's evaluation." Sergei balled his fingers into a fist. "Not once in his paper did he mention that your hiccups continued while you slept. What careless work. Such inexact reporting from a medical professional purported to be the preeminent genius of his generation. I told everyone who would listen about Alexander's carelessness. I carried his paper with me and described its corrigendum to random passersby on the street. I showed doctors and nurses, entire committees full of medical practitioners. In the end, my outcry fell on deaf ears. Alexander's paper was well received. It won awards. A new condition had been discovered. They call it Vlad's Syndrome."

Vladimir shifted uncomfortably in his seat. Suddenly, the reactions to his hiccups in the hospital corridors made sense.

"I knew the moment he published that paper that Alexander had to be punished. It became, to me, an inevitability," Sergei said. "At first I might have been satisfied with his dismissal from the hospital, perhaps even a waning of the medical community's esteem for his genius. As time passed, I began to daydream of his banishment to some foreign, dark and dreary land where he spoke nothing of the language and after years of constant misery and loneliness, Alexander became a drunkard, reviled by a throng of scurvy-laden locals who treated him as nothing more than the common village idiot. Children would chase him with sticks and old ladies would hurl soggy, pestilence-ridden produce at him.

"Oh, if only I'd conjured up some underhanded scheme to disgrace my rival. I had it within me to design a tragic end to his omnipresent dignity. Yet each time I sat down to plot and conspire, to develop ruses and strategize demeaning predicaments in which to thrust that priggish fiend, a lethargy would envelop me. My lack of enthusiasm became my downfall.

"I began waiting for God or fate or destiny — any of these phantasmic forces — to strike Alexander down. Each morning when I rose and read the newspaper, I searched the obituaries for news that he'd been felled by a random flying hockey puck or perhaps that he'd died in some humiliating accident in a roach-infested hotel room involving a belt hung from the ceiling, a hermaphroditic prostitute and a live farm animal. No such news ever came. Instead, a year and a half ago, an announcement appeared in the newspaper. Alexander and Asenka were to be married. After years apart, they'd rekindled their old flame following a chance meeting at an event celebrating Stalin's signing of the non-aggression pact with Germany. I couldn't help but be distraught. I looked at my child wailing under the kitchen table — eight years old and still an imbecile — my devoted spouse who couldn't string three sentences together and her senile mother tottering about in the background.

"I knew then that Alexander had to be destroyed.

"There comes a moment in every man's life, my boy, when you realize that scheming — the very act of planning your vengeance — will only lead to a lifetime of scheming and bear absolutely nothing: no glory, no embarrassment of riches, no fruits of your labor. Only he who acts will reap what he has sown.

"I stormed from my apartment and traveled to the hospital. The hour approached noon as I arrived at the staff cafeteria. There, sitting smugly at the end of a table eating a lunch of dried figs and ham was my nemesis Alexander. A tempest formed in my brain, with swirling black clouds and bright streaks of light. I stomped over to the cutlery bin and grabbed the sharpest knife I could find. My mind erupted in chaos. The world lay dead and black. I walked over to Alexander and, without even announcing myself, stabbed him in the side of the neck. He fell to the ground and I leapt upon him. Over and over I stabbed him. Blood spurted in living streams of red. Alexander was helpless to defend himself. Quickly bystanders intervened and I was thrust off his quivering body. An emergency bell sounded and swarms of doctors ran in to try to save him. They were helpless. He was too far gone. My enemy — the beast who'd ruined my life and perpetually plagued my nightmares — had finally been vanquished.

"I stood in front of the teeming mass of my former colleagues, my arms constrained and the knife ripped from my hand. Looking into their accusing eyes, I knew they would never understand that I'd been forced to do this, how in truth I had no other choice. The lot of them seemed about to lynch me when I did the only thing I could think to do.

"I hiccupped.

"A few seconds passed and then I hiccupped again. And again, just as I'd watched you hiccup, Vladimir, all those years ago.

"Whispers started almost immediately amongst the crowd.

"'Listen to him.'

"'Do you hear that?'

"'He has Vlad's Syndrome.'

"I kept hiccupping as the police came and arrested me. I sustained my ruse through a brief pretrial hearing during which a panel of psychologists determined that I did indeed have Vlad's Syndrome. Later, I continued my voluntary convulsions as they sealed me away in the psychiatric ward of what used to be my own hospital. I've kept hiccupping until this very day."

"But isn't it difficult to pretend to hiccup every waking hour of the day?" Vladimir said.

"Difficult? It's nearly impossible! But I've done it." Sergei nodded his head proudly. "I've fooled them all. Don't you see how brilliant it is?"

Vladimir shook his head.

"I've murdered my rival — a deceitful villain if ever there was one — and what's saved me from prison is the syndrome based on the lies he conjured up."

Vladimir couldn't hide his shock. He didn't quite know what to say. Doctor Namestikov had always seemed sound of mind. As a child, Vladimir could never have known that Sergei's rivalry with Alexander was burgeoning into the realm of obsession. He looked across the table and saw the mania in Sergei's eyes. Just minutes ago they appeared lifeless and dull. Now they darted about the room in hurried glances, never settling too long in one place.

"Is there anything I can do to help you?" Vladimir said.

Sergei recoiled in surprise. "Help me? Vladimir, I'm your doctor. I'm supposed to help you. Not the other way around."

Vladimir looked past Sergei at the drab, bloodstained walls illuminated by the flickering light. Had there been a window anywhere in this room, it most assuredly would have been sealed by thick iron bars. Vladimir's focus shifted to Sergei's emaciated cheeks, his long gray hair and the crazed white whiskers gushing from his chin. Despite his weight loss, his belly had distended. Sergei's nostrils had permanently swelled.

"Is there someone I can call for you? Markus perhaps?" Vladimir said.

"Markus?" Sergei smiled a little as he remembered his old friend. "No, no. Things did not end well between the two of us. I wouldn't want to have him visit me here. It's dreadfully difficult to invite a friend over for tea in this place, Vladimir. They hide me away and keep me in these." He held up his chains. "I'd rather not have Markus see me this way."

"Perhaps he could help."

Sergei nodded as though he agreed, but his eyes drifted in circles.

Vladimir leaned in close to whisper in Sergei's ear. "If you ask me to, I will get you out of here. This place isn't a real prison. I can break you out."

Sergei appeared to be considering Vladimir's proposal. Vladimir sat across from him, his heart racing. In truth, he wasn't sure he could pull off such a feat. He waited on Sergei's answer with bated breath.

"No," Sergei said. "I couldn't ask you to do that. I'm fine in here. I'll get the best of them yet, don't you worry."

"Is there anything I can bring you?"

"No."

"Some fruit maybe? A meal from a restaurant?"

"No."

"Some canned plums, perhaps?"

"No."

"A girl . . . you know, a prostitute?"

Sergei hesitated. "No. Thank you, but no."

Footsteps sounded down the hall. Vladimir stood up from the table.

"Will you be back to visit?" Sergei said.

"I will. I'll speak to the nurse's aide about a visit next month."

Vladimir said these words with conviction, but deep inside he wasn't sure. He'd survived a year in the wild and the lethal Waterfall of Ion. In the course of his twenty years, he'd been through a great deal. Despite his empathy for Sergei, Vladimir didn't know if he had the strength to see him again.

"Will you be leaving Moscow?" Sergei said.

"Yes," Vladimir said. "I'm going to visit my mother. It's been far too many years. I hope she's still alive."

Sergei's hiccups returned the moment Ilvana Strekov appeared at the door. He stood up and embraced Vladimir. His former patient could feel the skeletal outline of the doctor's ribs.

It was time to go.

"*Schastlivo ostavat'sya*," Vladimir said.

"Keep well," Sergei said, his voice cut with gravel.

Walking in small steps to facilitate his chains, Sergei stopped at the doorway and braced his arms against the entrance as though he were about to be pulled into an eddying whirlpool on the other side. He cast Vladimir a final desperate look. Then he disappeared.

fifteen

Ilvana and Vladimir stole quietly through vacant halls with Vladimir restraining his hiccups as best he could until they returned to the same spot in the courtyard where they'd met. She handed him a small rectangular package covered in brown paper and insisted he open it after he left. Vladimir tucked the package into the satchel containing all his belongings. An icy winter rain was blowing sideways in the wind. Careful not to step outside, Ilvana poked her head ever so slightly through the crack in the doorway.

"I'm curious," Vladimir said. "When I first arrived, Doctor Namestikov asked me whether I was here to kill him. Why would he say such a thing? Is there any truth to this?"

"The doctor has been very sick, Vladimir. You can't trust in what he says," the nurse's aide said. "Now listen to me very carefully. You can't stay in Moscow. You most definitely must stay away from the hospital. If anyone hears your hiccups, they'll lock you away just as they did Doctor Namestikov. You don't want that, Vladimir. Go back to your village. Live your life. Stay away from here until the end of the war. No good can come from you meddling in the doctor's affairs."

She went to shut the door. Vladimir stuck his foot in the entranceway to stop it from closing. He grabbed Ilvana by the wrist. "Promise that you will contact me if the doctor's condition changes," he said. "Please, I beg of you, if anything happens — send a telegram to the main post office in Igarka."

"I must go." Ilvana struggled to yank her arm free of Vladimir's grasp.

"Promise me."

"I'll scream," she said.

Vladimir let go and Ilvana Strekov recoiled into the hospital. The door closed between them. The last Vladimir saw of the woman, she was hurrying past a distant window with tears streaming down her face.

Vladimir turned and walked in the winter rain. At the hospital gates he reached into his satchel and pulled out the rectangular object Ilvana had given him. He tore the brown paper away. Wrapped in a piece of string were dozens of letters his mother had sent to him over the years. Still sealed, the envelopes had never been opened. Vladimir could picture his mother rocking on her chair in the sitting room, wearing her blue dress with the floral print around the collar. All these years, she'd been trying to reach him. She might think he's dead, or worse perhaps she thought he'd received her letters and didn't want to reply. A scattering of lights were on in the hospital windows at this hour. The building looked lifeless and frozen, brick and mortar and glass and nothing else. This wasn't Vladimir's home. Moscow wasn't where he was meant to be. He tucked the letters into his bag, turned from the hospital and began walking toward the train station.

For the first time in twelve years, Vladimir was headed home.

The snowdrifts in Igarka ranged from ankle-deep to waist-high. Vladimir marched through the interminable fields of white for almost two hours before he finally saw the old schoolhouse. It hadn't changed in twelve years. Small and dilapidated with endless passages of snow on all sides, it looked the part of a tiny ship foundering at sea with nary any land in sight. Vladimir stopped outside and thought of that mammoth man the Professor — how he always seemed to breathe through flared nostrils and the crisp, terse way his words flew out of his mouth. Vladimir walked up to the entranceway and stepped on his toes to peer through a tall window. He even considered knocking on the schoolhouse door, if only to see what a dozen years had done to the man. In the end, he decided against it. After all, what would he say? What had he ever had to say to that ill-tempered disciplinarian?

Vladimir turned and walked away from the schoolhouse and never gave the Professor another thought. He couldn't have known that at that very moment thousands of kilometers west in a tiny one-bedroom apartment overlooking the Atlantic Ocean, Urie Kochuokova was rubbing a circle of red paint on his nose and slipping into a jumpsuit dotted with a rainbow of colors, preparing to entertain a group of young children by twisting balloons into the shapes of squirrels and receiving an absurd number of pies in the face. Six years earlier the Professor had left his comfortable position as sole educator in the village for a career as a diplomat in Moscow, only to have every manner of vocational door slammed shut in his face. His dreams shattered, Urie Kochuokova had every intention of living out the rest of his days as a cantankerous old fart, spewing bile and decrying anything and everything that made others happy. On his fifty-third birthday, he purchased two jugs of vodka and staggered up to his apartment to drink himself to sleep. He consumed three quarters of one jug and an eighth of the other before passing out with his head in the kitchen sink. The Professor awoke the next morning to discover he had become an entirely different person. Whether his brain had been damaged or the gods had spoken to him, he didn't know, but in a stunning turnabout, the effects of that one night hard at the drink made him less volatile and more amiable than he'd ever been. He found himself prone to unpredictable fits of giggles. In the market, at the doctor's office, at his work and play, Urie Kochuokova saw only the joy in life. He married a lovely — though slightly pudgy — Norwegian woman and now spent six days a week performing professionally as *Борис Клоун* (Boris the Clown), renowned for his ability to contort his giant frame into unbelievably comical positions and, most importantly, to bring smiles to the faces of small children.

Past the schoolhouse and through the tall pine trees, Vladimir entered his sleepy village. A well of emotion overcame him when he saw the roof of his mother's house again. During the long journey to Igarka, Vladimir had sat in the train staring at the stack of unopened letters. He hesitated. He had what amounted to a third-grade education and didn't trust his ability to read what was inside. Twelve years ago, Sergei had been too concerned with curing Vladimir's hiccups to worry about tutoring the boy, and Gog, had he shown any desire to share his knowledge, was a poor grammarian himself. Vladimir had struggled to read even the simple note and map Gog left behind after his death.

The mechanics of Vladimir's thoughts, for so long fixated on the structure of words said aloud, were a kaleidoscope of symmetrical patterns — bright blues and iridescent oranges, sharp corners and spheres, lies told without malice and truths irrefutable. He had never been trained to arrange his emotions into orderly sentences. His thoughts compartmentalized into primordial urges — love, laugh, rage, kill. These words on a page, how others constructed their thoughts, were distinctly foreign to him.

On the train, Vladimir had summoned his resolve and opened the first letter, dated three days after he had left home. From what he could decipher, Ilga wrote about how greatly she missed her son and how much she loved him. Vladimir opened the next letter and the next. Their content was all the same. His mother would tell him how much she missed him. She would complain that Doctor Namestikov insisted she delay any visits for fear of setting back his patient's progress. Then she would tell Vladimir she loved him and sign *Mama* beside a small drawing of a heart. Over time, a disturbing trend emerged. About a year after Vladimir departed, Ilga's penmanship started to falter. Her words meandered. The characters lay scattered across the page, evidence of Ilga's shaking hand. With each passing year, Ilga's letters became less frequent and more difficult to understand, until eventually they became indecipherable altogether. The last letter was dated twelve months ago.

Vladimir approached his mother's house slowly. A thick layer of snow rested above a series of beveled icicles dangling from the roof. The entire structure looked smaller than it had when he was a child. Vladimir knocked on the front door. He knocked again and there was no answer. Gently, Vladimir tried the doorknob. The antique hinges creaked. "Hello?" he called. "Hello, Mother? It's me, Vladimir."

The living room looked unlived in. In the far corner, a three-stringed balalaika made of marbled wood lay against the wall. A bowl of decaying pears sat on the coffee table. Everything in the room was breathless and dead, as if just minutes ago the balalaika had been playing a cheery folk song while the pears danced in delight, only to have their merriment eradicated suddenly and tragically, leaving only sadness behind. It was cold inside, more so than out in the elements. Vladimir called for his mother. He walked into the kitchen and down the hall to her room. She wasn't there. Vladimir checked the bathroom and looked out the door into the backyard before heading down the hall to his old room. There, lying in a pile of blankets on Vladimir's old bed was his mother, Ilga. She absolutely dwarfed the child-sized mattress. Her legs dangled off the end and her torso filled its width. Ilga's face was bloated from years of alcohol abuse and her hair — always a matter of pride with the woman — had grown long, tattered and gray. A large pair of fox fur earmuffs covered either side of her head. She was clutching a small blue blanket and shivering in the cold.

Vladimir sat down next to her. "Mother?"

She didn't answer. Ilga's eyes were open. She appeared to be immersed in a lingering, motionless daydream.

Vladimir touched her shoulder.

Ilga looked up at her son. Her eyes grew wide. "Vladdy?" she said, still shivering.

Vladimir went to respond when Ilga shielded her face with her hands.

"No, this cannot be. You are the creature who haunts my dreams. You aren't real."

Vladimir took her hands. He wasn't sure whether Ilga could hear him through the fox fur. "It's really me. I'm not a boy anymore. I've become a man. I'm sorry I was gone so long, but now I'm here to take care of you."

Ilga sat up on the bed. She took Vladimir's face in her hands and rubbed her fingers along his jawline. A moment of pure elation overcame her. She smiled and tears flooded her eyes. Ilga wrapped her arms around Vladimir. "Oh, Vladdy," she said. "How I've dreamed of this day."

Vladimir removed his mother's earmuffs and felt the joy emanate from her like the rays of a small red sun.

It would not last the passing of 3.7 seconds.

Vladimir hiccupped.

Ilga recoiled from his embrace. "Vladimir?" she said. "Did they not cure you?"

"No, Mother. I still have the hiccups," he said.

"Oh God, no!" she cried. Ilga stood up, only to swoon back down. She burst into tears and started ranting hysterically. Vladimir tried to pacify her, but with each successive hiccup, she grew more and more frantic until eventually she collapsed back into bed in the exact position Vladimir had found her. This time Ilga fell into a deep sleep.

Vladimir placed a blanket over her shoulders and spent the next hour chopping wood in the backyard. He lit a fire in the central kitchen hearth and searched for something to cook. In the icebox were several leaves of cabbage. Vladimir boiled the cabbage and poured a stiff glass of vodka, then waited beside the bed for Ilga to awake. When she finally came to, a drowsy Ilga had regained her composure. Vladimir fed her the vodka. She gulped it down in one cathartic swig. The alcohol seemed to assuage her further and Ilga wanted to hold her son. Vladimir sat on the side of the bed with Ilga's arms wrapped tightly around his shoulders for nearly an hour. When Ilga finally let go, she followed Vladimir into the kitchen, where they sat down opposite one another at the table.

Vladimir gave a detailed account of the twelve years he'd been gone. Ilga seemed only to hear bits and pieces of what he said. When he finished, she told Vladimir that he had been on a great adventure and that he was special. Somehow she managed to ignore everything Vladimir told her about the wickedness that had once occupied his soul and the torturous nights he had spent storming aimlessly through the woods in Mongolia. She heard only that Vladimir was a great hunter and a traveler and marveled at what a handsome young man he'd grown up to be. Ilga even found it in herself to ignore his hiccups. It was like she convinced herself that each convulsive yelp wasn't really happening.

Somewhat reluctantly, Ilga in turn recounted what happened at home while Vladimir was away. Six months after Vladimir had gone to stay in Moscow, Ilga received word via the post that Vladimir's soldier father had gone missing somewhere near the Uzbekistan border. Initially, the Red Army declared him a missing soldier and stated that were he still to be a missing person in one year's time, he would be declared legally dead and Ilga would receive compensation from the government in the form of a lump-sum payment and a small amount paid per annum. Twelve months later, the first payment didn't arrive. In its stead, Ilga received a letter from the Committee for State Security stating that her husband's status had been redefined as Absent Without Leave. No money would be coming from the government. Ilga, upset over Vladimir's sudden affliction and herself developing the beginnings of severe arthritis in her hips and wrists, was powerless to dispute the Kremlin's declaration. She refused to accept that her husband was an army deserter. He would never abandon his country, let alone his wife and child. Ilga had held out hope that her husband would be discovered alive, perhaps as a prisoner of war. Later she prayed that they would find him dead, amongst a pile of rotting corpses or in a mass grave if need be, if only to assure her that he had been devout and valorous to the end.

Ultimately, the answer to his mysterious disappearance came from the dead man himself. Three years after he went missing, at a time in which Vladimir was already living with Gog in Mongolia, Ilga's husband sent her a parcel from Florence, Italy. The parcel contained monies in Russian funds and a terse, passionless letter stating that he had started a new family with a woman he'd met during the course of duty and the sum contained in the parcel would bring to a close their relationship as husband and wife. The amount was by no means insignificant but not particularly monumental either. No return address was given.

Ilga fell into a great depression. Her health steadily declined over the years. Her arthritis spread from her wrists to the rest of her body. For five years now she'd used a cane to walk. At first, Ilga hadn't visited Vladimir because Sergei was adamant that the presence of relatives would cause unexpected delays in her son's treatment. As one year turned into the next and the hospital stopped replying to her letters, Ilga longed to see her son. But the constant pain in her joints had grown to where even the simple act of walking was excruciating and she had come to fear the fire-like spark that ignited each time she stretched her feet.

"I haven't hardly felt the pain since you came home, Vladdy," she said.

Vladimir knew this wasn't true. He could see Ilga's teeth clench when she smiled and how she did everything she could to avoid wincing in front of her son. Her posture — the way she sat and moved and spoke — betrayed the severity of her condition. Vladimir couldn't help but wonder how things might have been different if he had stayed. How much of her ailment was caused by the anguish of him leaving? How would she look and feel now if Vladimir had never left?

He placed his face in his hands and swallowed hard. His

fingers slid above his hairline and pressed against his scalp. He looked down into his lap and then up to meet Ilga's gaze.

"I will take care of you now, Mother. I won't leave you again," Vladimir said.

Ilga smiled and cried. Together the two of them feasted in celebration on a dinner of *lenivye golubtsy* and slightly sour milk.

The next morning, Vladimir headed to the piers in Igarka to find himself gainful employment. He initially planned on working on a fishing vessel or perhaps at the docks, but the Yenisey River had almost frozen over and within a few weeks it would be closed to travel. Igarka was still quite a small town. Vladimir lived in a time long before the installation of the renowned permafrost museum or even the unsuccessful attempt to connect Igarka to the Russian railway network at Salekhard. The only occupations available to an uneducated man of his age were fisherman or logger. His hand forced, Vladimir applied at two of the three sawmills. The first sawmill foreman, a lofty beast with a short-cropped mustache and a round nose, broke into a fit of laughter when Vladimir told him that he'd been hiccupping for twelve years. He called in his friends to listen and they too made good fun out of his misfortune.

The second foreman — also with a short-cropped mustache, but much slighter in stature and with a pointed nose that tilted skyward — took pity on Vladimir and offered him a job cleaning up in the mill. Within a few hours of work, Vladimir noticed a rat scurrying behind a crate in the loading dock. The foreman told Vladimir they'd had a vermin problem for well over a year. "Those parasites bring in nothing but disease," the foreman said. "One of my men even died last winter from an infection caused by a rodent bite."

That evening, Vladimir waited until the last worker had left the sawmill before producing a small hatchet and a plastic bag. He turned out all of the lights in the mill and climbed atop a large tree stump. Vladimir closed his eyes and listened. It was just like in the jungle. He heard the rats shuffling their tiny feet. He felt their movement, sensed their presence behind walls and underneath the machinery.

They were everywhere.

And they were going to die.

When the foreman arrived the next morning, his sawmill was shrouded in quiet. The machines weren't running and his workers were nowhere to be found. He checked both levels before walking out to the dock. A throng of gaping onlookers were gathered in the back. The foreman asked what happened and in return he received an assembly line of horrified, cavernous stares. The foreman pushed his way to the front of the crowd. Standing before the assembled mass was a shirtless Vladimir. His hand held the bloody hatchet. His breath was short. Beside him a pile of dead rats was stacked waist-high; hundreds of them, killed in all manner of ways — decapitation, suffocation, split right through. Vladimir stood motionless, his expression blank. Every 3.7 seconds a hiccup emerged from his mouth.

A chill echoed down the foreman's spine. He took off his jacket and placed it on Vladimir's shoulders. "Let's get you out of the cold," he said. The man ordered one of the workers to escort Vladimir to the office and get him some warm milk. "And as to the rest of you," he said, his words fostering greater conviction as he spoke, "there is something to be learned from this young man. He took initiative. And he very well may have saved one of your lives today." The foreman headed back into the mill, leaving behind a speechless crowd and a pile of slaughtered rodents.

After two weeks, Vladimir had established a routine. He worked at the mill Monday through Saturday. The foreman arranged for a coworker who traveled by dogsled to pick Vladimir up every morning and transport him back to his sleepy village in the evenings as well. Sundays were spent doing odd jobs around the house and playing *svoyi koziri*, a two-person game of cards, with his mother. Since he had arrived, Ilga seemed to be in fine spirits and with each passing day her condition showed slight signs of improvement. On the second Friday following his homecoming, Vladimir received his first wages from the sawmill. The foreman threw in a little bit extra as compensation for exterminating the rats. Vladimir beamed with pride when the stack of bills was placed in his one hand and a cluster of coins in the other. It was the first time he had ever made his own money. Including what Gog had left him, Vladimir had enough money to support his mother through the winter. His mind swirled with all the good things he could do with his wages. He could buy Ilga a car so she no longer had to rely on the goodwill of her neighbors to bring food and supplies. One day he might even be able to convince her to travel to the large cities in the southwest and seek proper treatment for her swollen joints.

Yes, Vladimir had great plans for his money. But first he would feast. He had worked hard for two weeks and felt he'd earned himself a reward. Vladimir eschewed his ride home and headed over to the local alehouse for dinner. The tavern was a lively place, with sawmill workers and locals sharing tall glasses of beer and mingling with their friends. Full families, mothers and fathers, great aunts and their assorted offspring were enjoying meals in booths set up against the far wall, and next to the bar a husband-and-wife singing duo were performing an old Scandinavian folk song, the wife's voice high and pretty, the husband accompanying her on the accordion, his voice low and full of gravel. Vladimir tried his best to muffle his hiccups when he entered the pub. He walked through the clusters of people holding tall glasses of imperial stout and found an unoccupied booth toward the back.

His waitress, a pretty young thing not yet sixteen years old but with an ample, partially exposed bosom and long hair in curls, took his order. Vladimir ordered a glass of *Medovukha* and searched the menu. He could barely read some of the words.

"Is there a special?" he said.

"Yes. Would you like to hear about it?"

"No," Vladimir said. "Whatever it is, I'm sure it's very good. I'll have the special, please."

The evening's special turned out to be a green goulash with sautéed turnips. Vladimir dug in ravenously. He ate as though he'd been hungry for years. When he finished his meal, he ordered a glass of imperial stout and leaned back in his seat, comfortable and satiated. The singers had taken a break from performing and the chatter picked up in the alehouse. A hotly contested game of *gorodki* found a winner in the far corner. Vladimir was absently running his hand along the edge of his glass and dreaming of his newfound, modest wealth when he saw a vision out of the corner of his eye. It was that angelic little girl from long ago.

Vladimir would have recognized her anywhere. Ileana Berezovsky had grown up, of course. No longer was she that long-haired child with the slight shoulders and small hands.

She was a woman now. Her hair was blond and short, curled just behind her ears, and she was wearing purple mascara — a sign of the times, perhaps? Vladimir wasn't quite sure. But her features remained the same. She still had that tiny nose: pert and perfectly square on her face. Her eyes were as wide and beautiful as they'd always been. When she turned to speak with the waitress, Vladimir saw the profile of her heart-shaped lips, the ones that had enchanted him so long ago. After all this time she was still flawless and pure. Ileana was sitting amongst a crowd of seven — four men and three women — at a seat just a few meters away.

Vladimir couldn't help himself. He slid out of his booth and walked straight over to their table. He stood in front of Ileana, speechless and in utter adoration, hiccupping every 3.7 seconds.

Ileana looked up at him with those wide eyes. "Hello," she said.

Vladimir felt a flush of emotion in his chest. He tried to speak, only the words refused to leave his mouth. So he did the next best thing. He gazed upon her. He took in her every feature. He memorized the minutiae of her entire being, for if he were ever to be forced back into the Mongolian wild, with chaotic thoughts plaguing his troubled mind, he would have something new to hold on to.

Somehow Vladimir failed to notice the enormous thug with his arm around her.

The man stared Vladimir straight in the eye. "Who in the hell are you?" he said.

Vladimir glanced briefly at him and then turned his gaze back to Ileana. He couldn't move. He felt no other sensations — not the cold air seeping in through a crack in the nearby window nor the loud voices coming from all around the bar.

He breathed in fully and deeply. At last, after more than a decade of existing in ambrosial fragments in the corners of Vladimir's memory, that precious aroma made its way back to him. It was very faint and Vladimir had to decipher it from a mélange of other aromas floating through the air. But it was there. There was no denying it. Through the primordial odor of ripened cheese emanating from the floorboards and the ghastly gray-smelling cloud of smoke hovering in the air, beyond the baked pike perch and meat pies, the dried sweat in the patrons' armpits and the exhaust of dozens of mouths wet with a miscellany of sour wine and tangy Russian beer, Vladimir located that precious fragrance he remembered from his childhood — caramel and peaches outside on a spring day. It had been so long that he'd begun to believe he'd fashioned that smell out of nothingness. Here it existed as an irrefutable truth. Vladimir inhaled again and again. He filtered out the rubbish and drank in only Ileana's pure scent.

The colossal brute beside Ileana yelled at Vladimir. "What the devil do you think you're doing!?"

The other patrons, some sixty-three souls, reared their heads. The tavern fell suddenly quiet, leaving the hypnotic pulse of Vladimir's hiccups as the only sound.

The man stood up to face him.

Vladimir opened his eyes. He recognized this man at last. It was Pavel Discarov, the boy who had mercilessly whipped spitballs at young Vladimir's head in the schoolhouse. He was the one who had carried Ileana's books back and forth from school, the one with those shifty eyes, neither passionate nor cruel, yet somehow impossibly devious and dumb. The body around them had matured, but those eyes remained the same. Apparently he'd been carrying Ileana's books for her all these years.

A look of realization came over Discarov.

"It's really you, isn't it?" He turned to one of his companions. "I told you the rumors were true. Everyone, may I introduce you to Vladimir, the amazing hiccupping boy. Where have you been all these years, Vlad? Have you been hiccupping all this time?"

Vladimir tried to hold in his next hiccup but it came out all the same, only with added — regrettable — vigor.

"Ileana," Discarov said. "This *dolboyeb sukin syn* has been hiccupping for ten years. What's that been like for you, Vladimir? Does it help you with the ladies? Does it tickle their short, curly hairs?" he said to the raucous laughter of his friends. Discarov sat down and took a sip from his beer with a look of great satisfaction in his eyes.

Ileana was the only one not laughing. "Vladimir," she said, "is that really you?"

"Oh, it's the hiccupping boy, all right," Discarov said. "He sounds like a donkey to me. Ee-haw. Ee-haw."

Ileana leaned into Pavel's ear and whispered something, but his friends were so very amused and he was causing such a scene, he doubled his efforts.

"One of my friends at the sawmill told me all about your homecoming, Vlad. They said that you can't read or write. What have you been doing all these years that you haven't managed to learn how to read?"

Vladimir gave Discarov a look of abject hatred. Deep within, a red rage escalated. He glanced around. The entire bar had been drawn to the scene. They were all eagerly anticipating Vladimir's reply.

"I've become a hunter," Vladimir said. "I've killed all manner of beasts in faraway lands."

"Oh, I heard about that too." Discarov's voice dripped

with witless sarcasm. "I heard that you killed a pile of rats over at the mill. Is that what gets you off, rat-boy — stacking up piles of dead rats?"

Despite the lack of intellect or depth of wit behind his remarks, Discarov's friends broke out into a sea of hilarity. Never before had Vladimir been forced to match wits. He dreaded doing so. With his lack of education and inexperience at trading barbs, he would be destined to lose, even to an opponent as demonstrably unfunny as Discarov.

Vladimir gave Ileana a final look. He closed his eyes and breathed in her sweet smell one last time, then turned to walk back to his booth.

Discarov, however, was not done.

"Off he goes again," he cried. "Poor hiccupping Vladimir is heading back to his land of make-believe, where he bangs away on sheep and murders *indriks* for sport."

Ileana stood up and told Pavel to stop. Discarov grabbed her by the arm and yanked her back down into her seat.

Vladimir's eyes filled with fire. Needles shot through his arms. "Don't you hurt her," he said.

"She's not your girl," Discarov said, his hand still firmly gripping Ileana's arm. "So I fail to see how what I do is any concern of yours."

Vladimir looked at this brute's doltish expression, his thick square skull and the beginnings of a wart on his chin. With each passing moment Pavel Discarov tightened his grip on Ileana's arm, cutting off her circulation and turning her wrist purple with pain. Vladimir felt that familiar sensation, that violent green mixed with piercing red that used to stab through his brain at night. He could take it no longer.

"If you don't release her — I will kill you," Vladimir said.

sixteen

The two men circled one another in the ankle-deep snow outside. Around them, the bar patrons had turned into a pulsing throng of humanity. They cheered and cried out, some raised glasses of beer while others jostled for better position. Above, a light layer of snow descended in wide, sparse flakes, incongruous with the battle about to take place. Vladimir positioned his legs. He raised his fists in the air and stared into the hulking beast that Discarov had become. Pavel towered over Vladimir, his shoulders round and wide. His jaw had a thickness to it that suggested even a running thrust with a mallet would do no damage. Discarov raised his fists as well. Each was nearly the size of Vladimir's head.

In Vladimir's haste, in his anger, he'd neglected to take into account that while sitting down, Discarov had near equaled his height. He must have outweighed Vladimir by twenty-five kilos. Still, Vladimir stood his ground in the snow. The cries and jeers of Discarov's friends, the cacophony of noise from the bloodthirsty onlookers, even Ileana's pleas for the men to stop, melted into the Russian night. Vladimir was ready. He'd been ready for this his whole life. He stepped forward with clenched fists. Discarov cocked his arms. Vladimir was not afraid. David had his slingshot. Vladimir had his cunning, his passion, his rage.

He swung a wild punch at Discarov.

The man moved aside and Vladimir's punch sailed through

the air past the colossal brute. Vladimir lost his footing and turned around, trying to right himself. The last thing he saw was Discarov's fist driving into his face. Vladimir reeled. His jaw gave way and his legs turned to jelly. The world faded to black.

★ ★ ★

Vladimir came to slowly. The sudden unexpected unconsciousness was for a brief respite warm and comforting. Like the naked embrace of a devil-hearted woman who fears letting you go, the darkness held on longer than it had claim to him. Vladimir's eyes opened to see the black Russian sky dotted with fluttering flakes of snow. He tried to sit up, but his head hurt and his jaw was locked in place. The hiccups remained. Only now they hurt. A pang of pain shot along Vladimir's neck and jawline with each consecutive yelp.

A trio of concerned faces hovered over him. One was the female folksinger. Vladimir could see right up her nose. Beside her a gray-bearded man had a look of great concern and to that man's right was Ileana. She hadn't left. With the help of the bearded man, Vladimir sat up. Five meters away he could see the bar patrons filing back into the tavern, no doubt disappointed that his conflict with Discarov hadn't had more sport to it. Ileana was saying something. Vladimir reached up and cleared the snow out of his frozen eardrum.

"Are you okay?" she said again.

Vladimir tried to stand. The man helped him up by the elbow but he slipped and landed in the snow again. "I think I'm just going to sit here a while," Vladimir said.

The bearded man and the folksinger waited a few moments before succumbing to the cold and following the others back into the tavern. Vladimir cleared the snowflakes from atop his head.

"Where were you all this time?" Ileana said.

Vladimir reached into his pocket and put on his wool hat. He couldn't bring himself to tell her about the hospital, about Mongolia, about Gog and the Waterfall of Ion. "I was in Moscow, mostly," he said. "I left the country for a while too."

Ileana sat down beside him; she rested on one leg so as not to get her entire bottom wet in the snow. Since the moment she had seen Vladimir, she'd had a curious gaze on her face, the meaning of which Vladimir couldn't quite place. He knew nothing of women. The conversation with nurse's aide Strekov was the most he'd spoken to a woman in a decade. Ileana's voice was gentle and soft. In the distance the tavern door closed, and now it was the two old schoolmates sitting alone in the snow.

Vladimir rubbed his jaw with his hand. His legs still felt like two slabs of rubber. "I thought of you while I was away."

"Have you been hiccupping this whole time?" she said.

Vladimir nodded.

"Does it hurt?"

"It does since Pavel punched me in the face."

Ileana laughed. Vladimir laughed too, a short little chortle that caused his jaw to lock into place.

"Where are you staying?" she said.

"At my mother's house. She's been living here the entire time I was away."

"I know," Ileana said. "My aunt takes her bread and fish once a month."

"Are you married?" Vladimir said. It was an awkward statement, an assertion more than a question. Vladimir didn't know any better. He watched Ileana's shoulders stiffen, her slight smile flee her lips.

"Pavel and I are engaged," she said. "We're planning to move to Saint Petersburg. It's beautiful there, I've been told. Pavel has a cousin who settled down in Saint Petersburg a few years back. People say it's just like Western Europe, that it's more like living in Sweden or Finland than Moscow. There I might get a job in the war effort or perhaps go to school."

"But you're safe here. You're safe from the Nazis and the kamikazes."

Ileana shuffled her tongue along the inside of her mouth. "I'm not afraid of the Germans," she said and paused as if she were wondering whether or not she believed it. "I'm more afraid of never leaving this village, of never finding where I belong."

"When are you going?" Vladimir said.

"Soon. Maybe in the springtime. Within the year." A silence fell between them and hovered heavy in the night. Vladimir wished he'd known what to say. Ileana stood up. She brushed the snow off her leg. "I should head back inside." She turned to walk toward the tavern.

"Can I see you again?" Vladimir said.

Ileana stopped. "I'm engaged to marry Pavel."

"Not as lovers. As friends," Vladimir said. "I don't have any friends in Igarka. It's been so long since I was here. It would be nice to have someone to talk to, someone to have the occasional meal with."

She hesitated. "I don't know," she said.

"See me once before you leave then," he said. "Before you go away to Saint Petersburg and I never have a chance to see you again."

The lights from the tavern silhouetted Ileana from behind and Vladimir saw once again the profile of her face. It was still pristine, still unimaginably beautiful. He wanted this moment to last forever, he and the little girl in the sailor suit grown up, her figure in curves, her eyes wide and bright in the snow-covered night.

"This Sunday I'll be driving into town to buy groceries," she said. "You may accompany me if you wish. But only as a friend." Her voice stressed that point as though she were talking to a small child. "Only as a friend, do you understand?"

Vladimir nodded.

Ileana started walking backward toward the tavern. "I'll meet you outside the old schoolhouse at 9 a.m.," she said.

"I'll be there," he said.

"Don't be late."

"I won't." Vladimir's smile spread from ear to ear. He watched her walk up the stairs and open the tavern door. The revelry echoed out into the night.

"And, Vladimir," she said, "it's good to have you home."

seventeen

The next morning when Vladimir arrived at work, something seemed strange. He pulled up on the back of his coworker's dogsled, stepped into the shin-deep snow and stood in front of the mill to find it eerily quiet. Even at this early hour before the rise of the sun, the mill should have been a veritable hodgepodge of noises. The rackety old log loader, the four-sided canter with its malfunctioning linear positioners, the creaky vises and screeching saws, voices yelling up to the second floor and voices calling back down — it all added up to a blusterous roar.

This morning, Vladimir could have heard a cricket chirp. He and his coworker arrived twenty minutes late, their tardiness owing in large part to the injured leg of one of the lead sled dogs. Vladimir anticipated they would be the last ones in to work. He stood beside the injured husky and stroked it behind the ears. The animal nestled its nose into his hip and still Vladimir heard nothing from inside. The sled's driver, Anatoly, a toughened forty-three-year-old Tatarian skilled with a table saw, cast him an uneasy look as they approached the mill's central doors. Vladimir stepped inside to see the millworkers lined up alongside the far wall. Each of his compatriots had a grim look in his eyes. The lineup snaked all the way through the central floor and toward the foreman's office. Dutifully, Vladimir and Anatoly joined the back of the line.

"What's happening?" Vladimir whispered in one of the workers' ears. "Is the mill closing down?"

"That's the least of our worries," the worker said. The man stood on his toes and peered over his coworkers' heads. Vladimir did the same but couldn't see what was happening.

"The Red Army is here," the worker said.

"Why?"

"Conscription into the Great Patriotic War."

Vladimir was confused. "I'm not familiar with that word — conscription. Does it mean the same thing as genocide?"

The millworker shot him a foul sneer and turned back to stand in line.

Anatoly tapped Vladimir on the shoulder. "Conscription means that they're drafting us into the war. It's every Soviet male's holy duty to serve the motherland. We're going to be soldiers," he said. "We're going to fight the Germans."

Vladimir couldn't believe what he'd heard. He felt stunned. A sense of the surreal crept over him and suddenly everything and everyone in the mill looked pink. The flushed coral color radiated upward from the floorboards, dripped from the men's fingertips, hung like a coruscated mist in the air. The millworkers' downcast faces melted together into one sinister, frightful haze. Vladimir wiped his eyes. He stood on his toes again in an attempt to see the foreman's office and then looked back toward the mill's entranceway and wondered why no one had taken off running yet.

Anatoly's voice brought Vladimir back into reality. "You can't be surprised."

"I am," Vladimir said. "I'm very surprised."

Anatoly scratched his thick beard. He too eyeballed the front door. "I never believed conscription would happen so far north. Still, there've been rumblings about this for weeks."

"Well, no one told me."

The workers' heads all turned in unison to watch as two Russian soldiers, both young men no more than twenty-four years of age with pistols attached to their hips and steely looks in their eyes, walked in perfect step from the foreman's office, past the lineup of workers and toward the entranceway, where they loitered about, speaking in hushed whispers. Vladimir could only wait as the line moved forward. Every few minutes a new recruit would leave the office with a yellow envelope in his hand. Some of the draftees marched straight past the soldiers, through the doorway and out into the cold. Others returned to their work. Most were stoic, others grim. One young man couldn't help himself and broke into tears, his face red and purple, his mouth a quivering rectangle as he covered his eyes with his hands. Vladimir stood second to last in line as the numbers dwindled from over sixty, down to thirty, until just a handful remained, and finally Vladimir stood next to the closed office door.

It creaked open and another neophyte soldier brushed on by, yellow envelope in hand. A voice sounded inside.

"Next."

Vladimir entered the office. He'd expected to find the foreman inside, along with an entire committee of Russian generals clad in formal red attire, innumerable medals adorning their coats. Instead, he found a lone man wearing a green tunic with subdued collar tabs and a hidden buttoned front. Small, round glasses framed his face, and what a gaunt, yellowed face it was. The man's sunken eyes, his clean-shaven jaw that widened at the bottom to center his thin-lipped mouth, the premature gray hair protruding in slick slivers from under his military-issued cap — it all spoke of death. Vladimir felt as though he'd walked into a room and seen a corpse sitting behind the desk, calmly smoking a cigarette.

The man searched his list. "I only have two names left," he said. "Are you Vladimir or Anatoly?"

"Vladimir."

"Take a seat, young man."

As he sat down, the man checked Vladimir's name off his long list and pulled a piece of paper from a stack on the foreman's desk. He scribbled something down in black ink and then looked up.

"My name is Captain Karolek. I represent the 322nd Rifle Division of the 10th Army of the Soviet Union. The motherland calls you into duty." He paused to let the gravity of his words sink in. "Are you over seventeen years of age?"

"Yes," Vladimir said.

"Is there any disability, physical or otherwise, that would preclude you from active service?"

Vladimir didn't quite know what to say.

"Well, is there?"

"I have the hiccups."

"I know. I can hear that."

"No," Vladimir said. "You don't understand. I've had the hiccups for twelve years."

Captain Karolek set his paperwork aside. His eyes grew close together. "What did you say?"

Vladimir told him again how long he'd had the hiccups.

The captain extinguished his cigarette. He pulled out a thin metal case, lit another white Sobranie and leaned back in his chair. Captain Karolek turned his head to the side, squinted and arched his neck until he heard a loud crack. This captain, this cadaver come to life, lurched forward. He clasped his hands together. "Have you seen a doctor about your condition?"

"I spent several years in the hospital," Vladimir said.

"And they couldn't cure you?"

"No, sir."

"Captain," Karolek said.

"I'm sorry?"

"My rank is captain. As you're being inducted into the military, it is appropriate that you refer to me as Captain Karolek."

"No, Captain," Vladimir said. "They weren't able to cure me."

The man stood up from his chair and stretched, cigarette in hand. He walked around and sat down on the edge of the desk. His sudden informality surprised Vladimir. Karolek inhaled a long drag of smoke and exhaled it in consecutive circles, four in total, each wider and rounder than the last. When he was done, he fashioned a wry smile.

"I learned that trick from a composer I met in Moscow. I think his name was Prokofiev. Have you heard of him?"

Vladimir stared straight forward and hiccupped.

"No?" Karolek said. "He's quite highly regarded, I believe. Anyways, the man was sitting at a piano, tinkling the ivory keys in the high register with his right hand and all the while he was smoking with his left hand. He could blow seven or eight smoke rings from his lips in succession without ever losing his place in the music. Once the smoke was in the air, he set the cigarette down and struck the keys with both hands." As the captain shot his hands up in the air and brought them down swiftly to illustrate, Vladimir hiccupped again. It seemed to vex the man this time. Karolek paused to regain his composure and then continued. "It was a sound like no other I'd ever heard before. It was Russian music written by a Russian, played by a Russian under a red Moscow moon. I felt in that moment more patriotism than I've ever felt on the battlefield, more than I've ever derived from any of Stalin's rhetoric. The young people can have their Parnakhian jazz with those ear-splitting trumpets and saxophones. For me, the purest sound of this great nation will always be a man at a piano playing the music intended by our forefathers."

Vladimir stared at the man without the foggiest idea of what to say.

Karolek took a long drag off his cigarette and exhaled again. "I'm inclined to believe you when you say you've been hiccupping all this time. Quite frankly, it's too preposterous a story to just make up. Only I'm not quite sure what to do with you, Vladimir. A soldier simply can't make the noises you make. There is an element of stealth required in battle, even modern battle. If I were to assign you to my infantry division, you alone could cause the death of a hundred men. Perhaps more. By the same token, I'm loath to send you in on the first wave of an armed struggle. The men in the first wave rarely ever survive and that would seem unbearably cruel in your case — sending an invalid to the slaughter."

Vladimir was about to challenge this man's description of him as an invalid when he realized any objection would only serve to send him to the slaughter. He remained quiet.

"Do you have any skills that I don't know about?" Karolek said.

"I'm a hunter," Vladimir said.

"So you're adept with a rifle?"

"No. I hunt with a knife and a spear."

"Like a savage?" Karolek said.

"Yes, I suppose so."

"Efficiency with a spear is not a skill the Red Army is presently seeking. Do you have any medical expertise?"

"No."

"Are you a skilled chef?"

"Not really."

"Do you know anything about electronic devices? Are you well-versed in telegraphic communications code? Do you speak multiple languages or have any proficiency in mechanics?"

"No," Vladimir said.

Karolek stood up from the desk, walked around to the other side and sat down in the foreman's chair. He extinguished his cigarette and reached into his case to select another. "Then I'll have no choice but to send you into combat in one of our first-wave advances."

The room turned pink.

"Into the slaughter?"

Captain Karolek's sunken eyes peered at Vladimir over top of his round glasses. "Perhaps I've been too candid with you," he said and cleared his throat. "Giving one's life in the name of the motherland is the greatest honor to which a proud Soviet can aspire." Karolek reached up and took off his hat. He yanked his head sideways again, this time as hard as he could. Despite his best efforts, the vertebrae in his neck refused to cooperate. The crack never came and Vladimir could only sit and watch until Karolek finally relented. The captain composed himself and then handed Vladimir a yellow envelope, and when he did, Vladimir hiccupped. This involuntary eruption from his phrenic nerve — though very much identical to all of his other hiccups — seemed to affect Karolek. The man's eyes changed.

Vladimir moved to stand when Karolek spoke again.

"Wait. Sit. Please. I fear I've been hasty. My father was always hasty with me," he said. "As a result I grew up to hate the man with a vengeance. Now as to you, Vladimir, perhaps

I could assign you to our field artillery unit. This will allow you to be useful and at the same time keep you and your hiccups out of earshot of our enemy." Karolek looked at Vladimir expectantly. "Aren't you going to thank me?" he said.

"Yes. Thank you," Vladimir said. "Just one question — what is a field artillery unit?"

"You will be part of the team that fires our long-range weapons."

"So I'll be required to shoot bombs at German soldiers?"

"Artillery shells," Karolek said. "Not bombs, per se."

Vladimir shifted in his seat. "How will I know how many people I've killed?"

"The field artillery unit doesn't necessarily know how many targets they've neutralized. Regardless, the point is moot. This assignment is a good result for you. You should be happy. I would be happy if I were you." The captain smiled.

Vladimir smiled back, but in his stomach, he felt as though he were about to throw up. The very notion of killing other soldiers — innumerable men, by the sounds of it — sent a shockwave racing through Vladimir's entire body. He pictured the faces of the soldiers wounded but not killed by an artillery blast, their inflamed bodies writhing on the battlefield. It was all too much for him. Vladimir hiccupped. Three-point-seven seconds passed and then, unexpectedly, without warning, the next hiccup failed to arrive. That sense of the surreal increased tenfold. The pink cloud hanging over the room turned red. This had never happened before.

Vladimir sat in his chair, staring at Captain Karolek, dizzy and uncertain. Had his hiccups stopped? Was this the moment he'd been waiting for all these years? One second passed and then two and still nothing. Vladimir didn't know what to feel: joy, exhilaration, loss, anguish, bewilderment.

Another 1.7 seconds passed and then suddenly, like clock-work, Vladimir's hiccups returned to their metronome pulse.

The military captain was still staring at him, waiting for a response.

"Thank you," Vladimir warbled finally. He stood up to leave, yellow envelope in hand.

To his great surprise, Captain Karolek hurried around the desk and met him at the door.

"Be truthful with me now," he said. "Are you unwell?"

Vladimir hesitated.

"You strike me as a very ill young man," Karolek said, eliciting in his voice a tone of compassion for the first time since Vladimir entered the room. "Now I'm not apt to absolve a proud Russian from his nationalistic duty," he said. "But I'm also not the type of officer who would force a sick man into military service. So I ask you — are you well enough to serve your country?"

Vladimir just stared at the man, hiccupping, his eyes vacant.

"Here's what I'm going to do. And I must caution you that I haven't made an exception for anyone else. I'll put an asterisk beside your name. Tomorrow morning, all of the new recruits in Igarka are expected to report for duty at 8 a.m. in front of the alehouse across the way. If I see you there, I will understand you to be fit for duty and assign you to the field artillery unit of the 322nd Rifle Division of the 10th Army. If you are not there, I will declare you unfit for duty and relieve you of your responsibilities." He put his hand on Vladimir's shoulder and pulled him near.

Vladimir could smell the smoke on the captain's jacket. He saw up close the blackened pupils of the man's eyes.

"I know you will do what is right."

★ ✳ ★

Vladimir completed his shift at the mill in a daze. When it was over, he eschewed Anatoly's offer of a ride home and returned to the same alehouse where he'd seen Ileana the night before. Vladimir sat in the same seat, ordered the same green goulash from the same ripened young waitress with the curly black hair and kept his eyes on the door, hoping Ileana would enter so they might duplicate their chance encounter from the evening before. It took an hour and a half of sitting in the half-empty tavern, shoveling the goulash and turnips into his mouth and feeling anticipation transform into disappointment for Vladimir to realize that in life it's often impossible to repeat a moment and any attempt to force it into existence will serve only to tarnish the original moment's place in one's heart. The goulash — clearly reheated from last night's dinner and now covered in a milky blue film — tasted funny. The few scattered souls in the tavern spoke in muted tones. No doubt their loved ones were going off to war. Vladimir cursed himself for coming here.

He pictured himself just days from now, clad in full military attire with a gun strapped to his belt and a helmet protecting his head, loading an artillery weapon and pressing fire, the blast of the cannon, the missile shooting upward and disappearing into the sky, only to be followed seconds later by a far-off muted explosion and then the distant caterwauling of men's screams — men he would never know, men he would never meet face-to-face. Vladimir thought of Russia, his homeland, what Usurpet had said. This war had been started by an enemy force so corrupt and obscene that they aimed to annihilate an entire branch of the human race.

Could he really stand idly by and allow the Nazis to storm into his country and burn it to the ground?

Yet what about the hundreds of thousands of enemy soldiers caught in the quagmire? They couldn't all be driven by pure evil. He was sure of it. The German soldiers were men with families, with mothers, unwitting men like his comrade Anatoly or that poor soldier Vladimir had freed from the cage, good men forced into immoral misdeeds by their leaders. Would the greater good really be served by murdering these strangers? Would it be served by firing artillery shells like a coward who strikes from afar? Could Vladimir really leave his mother? And could he leave Ileana waiting for him in the snow on Sunday morning? Was he a coward to place these women above the needs of God and country or was it the bravest thing a man could do?

The waitress approached to take away what remained of Vladimir's goulash and sautéed turnips. She asked him if he wanted anything else and Vladimir couldn't speak. He stared at her pink eyebrows, the pink sheen cast over her hair, her plump pink bosom and the soft, quiet look on her face. Vladimir hiccupped and shook his head. The waitress removed his plate and walked away. Vladimir looked at the door one last time and then took his leave.

His walk home in the snow took over an hour. At the halfway point, the light snow drifting overhead turned into freezing rain. Vladimir's wool hat shielded him from the icy drops. He pulled his collar tight and soldiered on. Then a crackle sounded overhead. Vladimir looked into the distance. Black clouds had blocked out the last vestiges of starlight. A storm was edging its way toward his tiny village. Hail the size of marbles threatened to fall from the sky at any moment.

Vladimir picked up his pace. He made it home just as the freezing rain grew unbearable, moments before two thunderous bolts of lightning flashed across the sky.

As he opened the door, Vladimir was startled by a neighbor's cat darting out into the storm. His mother must have let it in earlier in the day and forgotten to let it out. He brought his hands up to his eyes. The animal's hair was all over the floor. Its dandruff, imperceptible to the naked eye, permeated the air nonetheless. Already it was causing Vladimir's eyes to itch. He made a mental note to sweep up after the cat and went to find his mother. She was sleeping soundly on Vladimir's bed, having forgotten to place a sheet over her shoulders. Vladimir picked up a blanket and wrapped it around her. He kissed her on the cheek and walked into the kitchen. Inside the icebox were three bottles of carbonated soda — locally distilled *kvass* really, refined from barley, yellow and sour-tasting. Vladimir had placed them in the icebox just that morning and tiny bits of ice had crystallized inside the liquid.

That bluish-green goulash wasn't sitting well. It had mixed with the sautéed turnips to form a nauseating stew in his stomach. Vladimir felt a murmur in his chest. When he tried to stand still, he almost toppled over backward. He braced himself and quickly downed two of the ice-cold beverages. Vladimir sneezed. That cursed cat. Vladimir walked back into the living room and removed his mother's broom from the closet. He started sweeping, his sneezes and hiccups alternating to make the task near impossible.

Vladimir set the broom down by the front door and there for the first time he noticed a small yellow envelope bearing his name on the front. In the bottom corner the word "TELEGRAM" was spelled out in large capital letters. It must have arrived while he was at work today. Vladimir tore it open to find a single sheet of paper. The typewritten note read as follows:

The doctor has asked me to pass on the following words — Ilvana Strekov

Vladimir, my boy. The time has come. My execution has been scheduled for this Sunday evening. I am helpless to save myself and have no doubt I will fall to the executioner's axe. I fear the dark unknown. Help me. Save me. Don't let me die. Your doctor, father and friend, Sergei Namestikov.

Vladimir couldn't believe what he'd read. He picked up the envelope and peered inside, hoping to discover a second note, something handwritten by Strekov, perhaps explaining the doctor's words away as paranoid folly. No such note existed. Only the plea for help.

That same churning nausea played again in Vladimir's stomach. His eyes itched. Vladimir thought of Sergei, the fear in his eyes as the executioner approached with his axe. He thought of the countless Germans he would be forced to kill. The walls of his house, the deluge of snow through the window, the very air looked pink. That murmur repeated in his chest. Vladimir picked up the third soda. He inhaled its contents in four swift swigs.

Then it happened.

Everything changed.

Vladimir felt a small twinge inside his intestines. It was short and more uncomfortable than painful. As if by instinct, Vladimir picked up the broom and continued sweeping. The twinge shuddered again. Vladimir looked down the hallway.

His mother was nowhere to be seen. He reached down and pulled his left buttock to the side. A long, loud spray of intestinal gas shot out. Vladimir's discomfort subsided and he continued sweeping when his insides tightened again. Simultaneously, the soda repeated on him. In the back of his mouth, the cat dandruff ignited a ticklish sensation. Vladimir felt it all coming at once. A belch formed in the base of his throat. Meanwhile the sneeze prickled in the meeting place of nasal passage and mouth. Down below, a second burst of gas readied itself.

He set down the broom and in one fell swoop, Vladimir belched, farted, sneezed, coughed and hiccupped all at once. The outpouring of gas and pathos was startling. Vladimir reeled. He dropped his broom and gripped the edges of a nearby chair.

Vladimir felt like he was floating above his body and could see the entire room, and the very next second his body went rigid. The blood in his veins turned to ice. The next hiccup, scheduled to arrive in its regular interval of 3.7 seconds, never came. Vladimir couldn't understand what was happening. A third consecutive hiccup failed to arrive as well, as did the one after that. He stumbled forward, his mind reeling. Vladimir looked around for something, someone, anything to explain to him what had just happened. In his throat, the phrenic nerve stood docile and still, unbothered by Vladimir's repetitive breaths.

The realization hit him like an automobile slamming into a cement wall. Vladimir had stopped hiccupping. The curse that had borne itself over and over again in his body for twelve long years was finally gone. Everything was so quiet. He looked down at the note again. Vladimir immediately forgot all about the army, about his holy patriotic duty. Doctor Namestikov was waiting for him, about to be executed, no less. Vladimir was the only one who could save the man. Yet the quiet, the stillness, the hush that had formed over the world, was unbearable.

For the first time, Vladimir feared he would lose all control.

Part
THree

eighteen

All around him, Vladimir heard the sounds he'd been impervious to for twelve full years. The creak of the boards as he
shuffled along the floor. The slow, methodical ticking of the
antique clock on the wall. His mother breathing in her sleep
from the room down the hall. The clatter of the world resonated for the first time and it was chaos. The sounds inside
the house came and went, banged and ticked, wheezed and
creaked as if Vladimir were made of stone, immovable,
immedicable, and the air was alive, throbbing like a thousand
overlapping heartbeats.

Vladimir ran to the back porch, stormed out into the cold
and fell to his knees in the snow. There he closed his eyes
and listened to the distant rumble of thunder, the hard rain
pelting down around him. Against the roof, it rattled. Each
successive drop landed in the snow like the muffled thud of
an anvil plummeting out of the sky. Vladimir couldn't take it.
He shoved his fingers into the back of his mouth in an effort
to make himself throw up, anything to shock his system and
make the hiccups return. It was no use. His stomach couldn't
be encouraged, not even if Vladimir had reached down his
throat with both hands and wrenched it into submission.

Vladimir's body felt like it belonged to someone else. The
air and the snow turned black and Vladimir knew not where
he was nor where he'd been, he knew nothing of this life and
the Earth, only the unnerving absence of light. Everything

disappeared and Vladimir wondered, *Is this death? Is this the end of everything I will ever know? If it is, why can I still think? How do I still know I'm here?* Wasn't this the cruelest trick of all, to be alive but dead, to exist on a plane of transcendental knowing and yet be unable to move, unable to feel the air against his face, unable to reach out and touch a blistered finger to the world?

Like a vortex, the blackness collapsed in on itself. Outside in the snow, the entire world evaporated and then materialized suddenly back into being. A sound rang out in Vladimir's ears, a whoosh that started as loud as anything he'd ever heard, swelled even louder and then stopped, leaving emptiness to resonate. Vladimir was on his knees in his mother's backyard. He was alive — dizzy and reeling, disoriented and nauseous, but alive.

He stood up quickly, suddenly. Some manner of beast was approaching, a tiger or a panther. He listened more closely to the heavy thud of paws stepping through the snow, to each syrupy breath the animal took as it stalked its prey. Vladimir turned and readied himself to be attacked.

Standing in front of him was the neighbor's small orange cat. It stretched its back and meowed. Vladimir, bubbling with panic, hurried back inside. He slammed the door shut and locked it, then ran to the window and peered back at that orange cat standing in the snow. Its yellow eyes glistened. Vladimir couldn't shake the feeling that it had come to kill him. Was it completely implausible that this creature could be a demon from the netherworld? Certainly it was at least possible. Countless ancient stories exist about evil spirits and mischievous hobgoblins taking animal form on Earth. How could Vladimir trust that this wasn't the case? Would a common house cat walk in the snow? Would it sneak into your dwelling to plan your demise while you're not at home and then run away like a cowardly beast when you finally enter through the door?

This thing, this demon, had come to kill Vladimir. He knew it now. It had started by deploying its dandruff to make his eyes itch. Now the cat had returned to finish the job.

Vladimir wouldn't let it happen.

He searched the kitchen like a madman.

Vladimir found a meat cleaver over by the cupboards and stormed out the door. He screamed a guttural scream and lunged into the snow. The cleaver sailed through the frozen rain. At the last moment the cat jumped out of the way. It scurried over to the porch with Vladimir in swift pursuit, grasping the cleaver like a bedlamite and bellowing into the night. The cat made a quick escape onto the neighbor's fence and off into the dark.

Vladimir pursued it to the fence and no farther. He knew exactly what was going on. The feline was trying to trick him! This whole business about entering Vladimir's home had been an elaborate ruse to convince Vladimir to leave the safety of his property and enter his neighbor's house, where his neighbor ruled the roost, where his neighbor could kill Vladimir sadistically and with complete moral and legal impunity. Well, Vladimir was too smart for that. He wouldn't enter through the backyard. He would barge straight through the front door and swing his cleaver at everything and anything that moved. Vladimir stormed toward the gate at the side of the house when his mother appeared at the door.

"Vladdy," she said. "What are you doing out here?"

"Go inside!"

"You'll catch your death of cold," she said.

Vladimir stopped in his tracks. Just like when he was a little boy, his mother was the voice of reason in this treacherous world. He stormed back into the house and dragged Ilga with him. Vladimir locked the door and peered outside again.

"Vladdy," she said.

"Hush."

"Vladdy," she said again. "Your hiccups — they're gone!"

"Yes, Mother." He closed the curtains and shot a look across the room. "They stopped a few minutes ago."

"This is a miracle!" she exclaimed. "What a joyous occasion. We must celebrate." Ilga stopped suddenly. Her eyes shifted to Vladimir's hand. "What are you doing with that knife?"

Vladimir looked down at the meat cleaver. He tossed it into the sink and marched toward her. "Do we have a gun in the house?" he said.

Ilga's eyes grew wide. Her mouth gaped open, quivered.

Vladimir grabbed her by the shoulders. He shook the old woman. "A gun!" he said. "Do we have a gun?"

"Yes."

"Where?"

"Behind the boxes in the hallway closet."

Vladimir pushed his mother aside and stormed down the hall. He flung the closet door open and tossed boxes into the air. Clothes and keepsakes tumbled onto the floor. Vladimir reached into the back and pulled out his father's old Nagant M1895 revolver. A seven-shot, gas-sealed gun; this relic from the First Great War had been his father's pride and joy. At the age of five, Vladimir's father had taken him to shoot at cans in the woods. Vladimir still remembered the feeling of cold steel in his hand, the powerful kickback of the gun, the warmth of the shell casings when he pulled them from the discharged weapon. He turned the chamber and rolled the barrel.

"Where are the bullets?" he yelled down the hall.

Ilga was standing in partial view in the kitchen alcove, her face riddled with shock.

Vladimir stormed back into the kitchen. He waved the revolver in the air. "Father kept boxes of bullets in the house. What did you do with them?" he said.

She started to cry. "I sold them years ago to pay for food."

Vladimir looked at her in disbelief. "Why did you keep the gun if you sold the bullets?"

"I kept it in case your father came home," she said. "He never did."

Vladimir watched the tears stream down his mother's face. He could feel her heart breaking from across the room. Vladimir walked over and wrapped his arms around his mother. "It's okay, Mama. I'm sorry. I got confused and excited for a minute. But there's nothing to worry about anymore. Let's get you some tea," he said.

Ilga heaved a low wail into her son's chest and allowed him to sit her down at the kitchen table. Vladimir was having trouble focusing. He'd already forgotten what he was looking for. "The tea," he remembered. Vladimir opened the cupboards and searched for the tea leaves. If he concentrated and focused all of his energy, he could complete this one simple task. Once his mother settled down, then he could decide what to do about Doctor Namestikov. He reached into the cupboard and found a jar marked *Tea*. Vladimir opened the jar and brought it to his nose.

Then the house came under attack.

Vladimir ducked. He looked up at the ceiling and ducked again. The world was ending outside. "What is that?" he said. "What's that noise?" Thousands of small collisions reverberated off the ceiling. Vladimir's mind went wild. The government had come to shoot him. Somehow they'd learned of his plan to save Doctor Namestikov and had tracked the doctor's telegram to this address. Captain Karolek's squadron was outside now, spraying gunfire against the roof in the hope that one lucky bullet would find its mark. Well, they wouldn't be so lucky. Vladimir picked up one of Ilga's cooking pans and held it over his head.

"It's hail," Ilga said.

Vladimir shot her an unglued glare. "What do you mean?"

"The rain turned to hail. There's a storm settling in. It's just the elements, Vladimir."

Slowly and with great caution, he parted the curtains and looked into the backyard. His mother was right. Hail the size of marbles was falling down all around the house. Vladimir tossed the cooking pan into the sink alongside the meat cleaver.

He paused and tried to breathe deeply. Vladimir thought of Sergei, how years ago his doctor had taken him from the ramshackle medical room in Igarka and placed him under his care in the hospital. Vladimir would have died without him. The last time Vladimir saw Sergei, the doctor's arms had looked frail, and a wild beard jutted out from his chin like a patch of weeds. Those shifting eyes. Vladimir had to do something. He couldn't just let Sergei die.

Vladimir ran to the front hall and picked up his jacket. He wrapped it over his shoulders and donned his wool cap as well. Vladimir had already opened the front door when he realized he would need money. He ran down the hall to his room and opened his top bureau drawer. Vladimir placed the clip of rubles inside his jacket pocket and retrieved the bullet-less gun from the counter. At the front door, he took one last look at his mother sitting in her kitchen chair, still waiting for tea.

"I won't be gone long. And when I return, I'll never leave you again," he said and ran out into the storm.

nineteen

The sounds of a train, perceived from within the belly of the beast, are nothing short of horrific. Vladimir didn't hear them so much as he felt them in his bones — the sporadic clanks and routine but often disarming screeching of the wheels as they navigated the tracks; the rattles and whirls that seeped from the windows, seats and floorboards; and deep within the locomotive, the endless chugging of the engine pulsing like an incised artery. Vladimir sat in his seat, hands firmly positioned over his ears, legs tucked up in an effort to conceal his body and make the world go away.

Hours ago Vladimir had stepped off the deck of a fishing boat that had just steered its way through boulder-sized chunks of ice along the Yenisey River. One of the fishermen, a foul-smelling man with three yellow teeth and an overcoat covered in fish entrails, told him that this would be their last trip for a month. "The river should have frozen over by now," he said. "You might find yourself having trouble getting home." Vladimir thought it was a miracle to even be alive after that harrowing journey. The constant swaying back and forth, the unstable floorboards that seemed ready at any moment to collapse into the river's fierce waiting arms, the odor of thousands of dead fish — it was all too much for him. Fifteen minutes after he boarded the boat, Vladimir leaned his head over the rail and deposited the green goulash overboard. The Yenisey River swallowed it up and gazed back at him for more.

Vladimir had hoped the tempest inside his mind would quell once he stepped off the boat. The hail had stopped altogether by the time they docked and he seemed to have escaped the black clouds of night. Dawn was rising. Vladimir fooled himself into believing the mechanics of the locomotive would purr him to sleep. They might have too, if not for the various odors in his assigned train car. They were another world altogether. With his hiccups gone, Vladimir's sense of smell magnified a hundred times over. Like a blind man in his seventh month without vision, he could smell the previous hundred passengers to have set foot in this small cabin for two. He smelled their sweat, their egg and cheese sandwiches, their perfumes, their seminal fluid and blood and lice and everything in between.

Vladimir looked at the clock on the wall. Forty minutes remained on his journey. He shut his window blind to keep out the burgeoning day and plugged his nose. Vladimir began counting the seconds until the train reached Moscow and he could finally escape into an open field and lie down on the snow-covered grass and pass out for an hour. The stillness of the white winter might save him yet.

But what about Doctor Namestikov? Vladimir couldn't forget why he'd traveled so far. The state was coming to kill Sergei. His doctor had asked for him by name. Vladimir placed his hand on the empty revolver in his breast pocket. Somehow he would have to procure some bullets and arrange a plan to save Sergei. Co-conspirators were needed, at the very least to provide a diversion; in a perfect scenario where they stormed the hospital gates waving burning planks of wood and pitchforks in the air. Vladimir's mind struggled to focus. Not just any plan would suffice. He needed something brilliant. If only it were him scheduled to be executed and not his beloved doctor. Sergei Namestikov would save him for sure.

Suddenly the door clicked open. Vladimir shot his legs out and sat straight up as a tall, thin Russian police officer entered the cabin. Vladimir immediately thought he was going to be arrested. Who had given him up to the Kremlin? he wondered. Was it his mother? That brute Discarov? That traitorous orange cat?

"Good morning," the man said. He sat down in the seat opposite Vladimir, unfolded a pair of reading glasses, placed them on the bridge of his nose and began absently flipping through the pages of his morning paper. Vladimir waited, his eyes fixated on the police officer. Was he playing some kind of game? Was he waiting for Vladimir to make the first move? Because he would. He very well could. In mere seconds Vladimir could remove the weapon from his jacket and bash the officer into submission. Or was this lawman simply sitting in the cabin, reading his newspaper and waiting for the train to stop?

Vladimir listened to the man's short swift breaths. The police officer seemed to suffer from a physical disorder of the nose. The sheer amount and force of oxygen he expelled from his left nostril dwarfed what the right nostril could ever hope to generate. Despite its unevenness, Vladimir found this noise peaceful. Every few seconds the man was sure to breathe out again, and Vladimir found he could tune his entire body to its rhythm. It would have been a perfect way to end the journey if the man hadn't insisted on talking.

"Traveling to Moscow today?" he said.

"Yes," Vladimir said.

The man set his paper down and lit a cigarette. "What type of business are you on?"

"I'm visiting a friend," Vladimir said, in effect imparting an imperfect truth.

"I just got back from visiting my father," the police officer said. "It's such a great shame to watch your parents get old. But I suppose they watched their parents get old and die and so did the generation before that."

Vladimir noticed the man looking at him strangely. A few uncomfortable seconds passed before Vladimir realized that in this social situation, it was customary for him to speak next. He racked his brain for the proper words. "And so did the monkeys before them."

"I beg your pardon?" he said.

"My doctor told me about it as a boy," Vladimir said. "The evolution of the species. How we grew out of monkeys hundreds of thousands of years ago. Our great-great-great-great-grandparents were monkeys. They swung from trees and ate bananas and threw their feces at one another. It's a scientific fact."

The man leaned forward. He crossed his eyebrows. "Are you a Christian man?"

Vladimir gave him a confused look.

"Do you believe in Jesus Christ as our Lord and Savior?"

"I don't suppose I've ever given it much thought," Vladimir said.

"Perhaps you should."

"You want me to consider this right now?" Vladimir said. In the back of his mind, he cursed himself for not beating a hasty retreat the moment this man had set foot in his cabin. Now, on top of the startling sounds and smells inside this cabin, his brain was forced to ponder the greatest theological question of all time.

"What better time than the present?" the officer said and returned to reading his newspaper. He huffed through his deviated septum, mumbled the word "monkeys" under his breath and flipped the page to the contemporary arts and dance section.

Vladimir stepped off the train and walked to the recently completed Krasnye Vorota Metro Station. The armed military presence had increased at the station. A checkpoint was set up with dozens of soldiers searching bags and inspecting passengers' identification. Instantly Vladimir worried that they would confiscate his weapon and arrest him. With a nervous perspiration building in his armpits, he presented the deceased soldier's papers and, to his surprise, the soldiers allowed him to bypass the line. He entered the central circular tunnel and found a map on the wall. That conversation on the locomotive had almost been the end of him. He couldn't imagine the horror that would accompany asking someone for directions. Vladimir stared at the map for what seemed an eternity before deciding to take the Metro north. He paid forty-five kopecks, a discount of five being that it was after the noon hour, and took the Metro three stops. The last station was one stop past his destination and, rather than return to the Metro with its guarded entranceways and cruel and confusing checkered floor pattern, he decided to walk the distance back to Sergei's hospital.

Moscow had transformed in the weeks that he'd been gone. Everywhere Vladimir looked he saw the war. Tanks lined the streets. Aircraft peppered the skies and soldiers were everywhere, thousands of them. They gathered in cafés, congregated in alleyways and marched in step down boulevards. Vladimir kept his head down and walked as fast as he could in the direction of the hospital. As he approached the gates, he saw two armed soldiers standing guard.

Vladimir hovered on the sidewalk across the street.

The clouds in the sky had returned, this time in the shapes of gray pieces of dough. The storm was gone but still his mind ached as though it were being pricked with needles. Each stabbing sensation came as an unexpected assault. The blood pulsing through his veins, his very breath, now felt wrong to him. Vladimir slumped down against the wall across from the hospital gates, only to realize that he must have looked like a beggar pleading for spare coins. Vladimir feared that some kindhearted woman would pass by and take pity on him. Her spare kopecks would slip out of her arthritic hands and land all over the sidewalk, where they would clatter and clang. All manner of well-bred citizens in the vicinity would look his way and condemn him for vagrancy.

Vladimir stood up. He clutched the empty gun in his jacket pocket and gazed at the hospital's mental health ward. The sparse windows were shielded by bars. Orderlies with hefty shoulder muscles patrolled the halls. Now armed guards surveilled the gates. An executioner was no doubt on his way with all manner of knives, nooses and scaffolds. Vladimir could never do this alone. That nurse's aide Strekov might be able to get him in the building, but then what? Who would procure a getaway vehicle? Who would drive the thing? Surely not Vladimir. He would steer it straight into a brick wall.

Vladimir needed someone to help him.

But who?

twenty

The lake was still. Afin, Sergei's former driver, the reformed butcher of Moscow, tugged on his fishing line. He really hadn't expected to catch any fish. A good portion of the lake was frozen over. Long thin sheets of ice formed symmetrical patterns above the water, and Afin had to thrash about with the oars to clear room just to traverse to the center. Now he sat in the cold, a flask of imperial vodka in his one hand, a fishing rod in the other. As dusk settled early, the stars in the sky appeared scattershot. From his vantage not even a single constellation held firm. Afin pulled in his line, slipped another frozen worm onto the hook and recast.

The years had caught up with him. His back ached. His neck was largely immobile. He could stare straight forward without discomfort, but turning to the side sent shivers of pain down his shoulders. No longer was he fit to drive a car. Afin's chin hung low like that of a defrocked Catholic priest. He knew well the job tasked upon him. Men in suits had made it perfectly clear. Men in suits hid their intentions behind formality and rules. They masked their evil well. At least thieves and murderers sometimes admitted to themselves what they were doing was wrong.

Nevertheless, the hour drew near.

He'd once been such a nice little boy. Could he really have changed so much from his days as a child casting stones across his lake back home? Afin picked up his oars and started back for shore. The time for peace in his soul had expired.

twenty-one

"You're a tricky sort, I'll give you that," Markus said. Eleven seconds earlier he'd opened an envelope and read a letter containing a single sentence — "Bishop to Queen 4." Markus shuffled over to the chessboard at the far corner of his office and moved the black bishop. He stared down at the pieces that remained. His pawns were decimated. He had no knights, only rooks and bishops left to protect his king. To an uneducated observer, it might have seemed like he had a fighting chance. In truth, Markus knew the situation was much more dire.

Months ago, when they had first begun exchanging letters, Professor Tillberry had backed himself into a corner. He'd opened, as expected, with the Sicilian Defense. That was brave of him, Markus thought. Tillberry's black pieces were laying claim to the center of the board and Markus's own white army would have to be equally as aggressive lest they surrender complete control. Soon enough, though, Tillberry had a crisis of conscience. After implementing the Najdorf Variation, essentially applying relentless pressure to White's pawn at King 4 — a course of action that was not only completely expected but almost a virtual certainty (Markus would have bet his soul on his opponent's fifth through seventh moves) — Tillberry relented and momentarily backed away. It was a simple move, receding his knight back into the king's fold. But it was cowardly as well. Markus took over.

He dominated. Tillberry's pawns fell like infantry storming blind onto a beach with no hope of ever making it to dry land. Markus was in complete control. What a fool Tillberry had been.

Now Markus wasn't so sure. Could his opponent have been lulling him into a false sense of security all along? Was this latest move a blatant act of folly or the most clever showing of gamesmanship to which Markus had ever been privy? And what on Earth had happened to his white knights? They were there just a few weeks ago. How could he remember the beginning and the end but nothing of the middle?

Markus smiled and angled the black knight to face due north. It was dark outside, evening having commenced before the dinner hour on this winter day. He stretched his short arms in the air and returned his misshapen hands to the safe embrace of his canes. "Ah, Tillberry, you are a problem for another day," he said and turned to leave his office.

Standing in his open doorway was the dark figure of a man with wide white eyes, his wool cap and coat damp from the day's rain. Markus stopped dead in his tracks. A dreadful fright shot through his body. He'd always known this day would come. He would have recognized this dark figure anywhere. The devil child had grown into a man. The hiccupping — that infernal yelp that had seemed incurable for so long — had disappeared. Still Markus had no doubt.

It was Sergei's protégé.

At long last Vladimir had come to kill him.

In a sudden, awkward shuffling of his feet, Markus turned and ran back toward his desk. His right cane lost its grip on the hardwood floor and Markus tumbled to the ground. He struggled to stand up. His right hand, with just the partial thumb and index finger, grabbed hold of an office chair. He flashed a quick look at that dark figure standing in his doorway. Vladimir had yet to move. Markus fumbled for his keys, found the short brass one and pushed it into the desk drawer. He pulled out a Webley Break-Top Revolver, the standard-issue service pistol for the armed forces of the United Kingdom. It was lighter than usual. "Curses," Markus muttered. He'd taken it out to clean it just two months ago and had forgotten to replace the bullets.

He pointed the empty gun at Vladimir.

"I always knew you'd come for me," Markus said. His useless right hand fished through the drawer for the bullets. Vladimir reached into his jacket and pointed a gun at Markus.

Markus froze in terror.

The room fell silent.

Vladimir's dark eyes hadn't changed. His stare was as vacuous as ever. Only now he towered in the air. Markus knew instantly that there would be no reasoning with him, no truce, no negotiation. Slowly he set the gun down on the desk. He closed his eyes and thought about his parents, the brother he'd wronged all those years ago. How could he, a man of so few options, not be expected to bed his brother's wife? For Christ's sake, she propositioned him, she seduced him, she ravaged Markus in the back seat of a trolley car. He pushed his brother's adulterous bride out of his brain. One's last thoughts should be of something good and pure. The taste of pink lemonade on the first day of spring. Caramelized apples. The smell of mint.

"If you're going to do it, be quick about it," he said.

Markus braced himself. Vladimir still hadn't moved.

"Blast you and blast Sergei for releasing your curse upon me!" he said.

To Markus's surprise, Vladimir lowered his gun.

He stepped forward.

The dwarfling flinched.

"I don't understand the language you're speaking," Vladimir said.

Markus's ears perked. Suddenly he realized he'd been yelling at Vladimir in his native English. The boy must have thought it was complete nonsense. Markus paused. He knew this type of criminal mind. He'd seen it throughout his practice over the years. Vladimir wanted to taunt him. He wanted to engage him in conversation and then launch into a long, drawn-out monologue before finally carrying out his nefarious deeds. And Markus, without a single bullet to fire, was powerless to refuse.

"What do you want?" he said in Russian.

Vladimir removed his wool cap and placed his gun on the table. "I need your help," he said.

twenty-two

"Vladimir?"

"Vladimir?"

Vladimir looked up from his seat in the lobby of Markus's office. Hovering in the air was the pointed, thin face of Ilvana Strekov. To her side was Markus. Ilvana's eyes were slightly droopy. She had her hand on Vladimir's shoulder and had been shaking him gently. Markus, for his part, was tapping one of his canes against Vladimir's shin. Each successive strike carried with it a little more force.

"Stop," Vladimir whispered under his breath.

Markus hauled back and delivered one final strike right on the bone.

"Stop!" Vladimir screamed. He grabbed Markus's cane and pushed Ilvana's hand away. The two medical professionals stepped back as Vladimir stood up. He shook his head. "What happened?"

"You were frantic when you entered my office. We practiced breathing exercises to get you to calm down," Markus said. "It took a while but finally you told me about Sergei. When I think about how angry I was at him all these years, when I think about what became of him, it makes me ill. I called the hospital and found your nurse's aide."

"We haven't much time," Ilvana said. In her hands was a warm beverage undoubtedly overflowing with caffeine. She took a swift gulp and her eyes rose above half-mast.

"When I let Ilvana into the office, you were catatonic on the couch," Markus said. "We've been trying to get your attention for a while now." He glanced up at the clock on the wall. It was nearly 10 p.m.

Markus said something else about time, about haste, about having to hurry, but Vladimir couldn't make out the words. Ilvana was speaking simultaneously and their two voices co-mingled in his ears. Vladimir faltered on his feet. The shadows danced in mesmerizing, rampageous circles on the walls. A loss of balance overcame him. He fell forward, straight into the arms of Markus. The diminutive man tried to catch him but wilted like a fossilized fern, and together they collapsed onto the floor. Vladimir could feel Markus's breath on his face. A pressure built up in the base of his throat. Vladimir wanted nothing more than to hiccup, to feel the sweet release. He swallowed and pushed the air to the base of his tongue but nothing emerged. Vladimir rolled off Markus and lay on his back, staring at the ceiling.

Ilvana tried to help him up. "You smell like fish," she said.

"I was on a boat. And then a train," Vladimir said. "I didn't have time to take a bath."

"What happened?" she said. "What's wrong with you?"

Vladimir looked into her meek eyes, biting her bottom lip in that timid way of hers. He could never expect Ilvana to comprehend how it had felt the moment the hiccups stopped. She'd never understand the cat that tried to murder him, the boat trip down the river or the noises on that train; how Vladimir stole through the streets in a desperate search for Markus's office; the paralyzing sounds of the appetent Moscow night. Vladimir pulled himself up.

"Doctor Namestikov is in danger," he said as calmly as he could. "Do you know when he's scheduled to be executed?"

Ilvana lowered her eyes. "Tonight at 11 p.m."

"But the time is almost upon us!" He turned to Markus. "What's our plan?"

"Plan?" Markus said.

"Yes. Our plan to save Doctor Namestikov."

Markus's voice was incredulous. "I haven't had time to devise a plan," he said. "This isn't really my realm of expertise, Vladimir. I'm not accustomed to great prison escapes or daring train robberies. I'm a psychologist, not a criminal mastermind."

"But we have to do something."

"What can the three of us truly accomplish?"

Vladimir looked at Markus with his stunted legs and his misshapen hands. He appeared to rely on his canes even more heavily than he had twelve years ago. Vladimir's eyes swung over to Ilvana with her frail arms and mouth cemented in the halfway point of sleep. She was almost out on her feet. He touched his head and the world swirled, glistening as though it were composed of hundreds of thousands of tiny mirrors.

Markus was right. What hope did the three of them have?

"No," Vladimir said. "I refuse to believe it. The hospital is not a prison. It is a hospital, nothing more. I don't care if the world is at war. I don't care if they shoot me like a dog. Doctor Namestikov would do everything in his power to save me if I were in his place. I just know it." He rushed over to the desk and picked up his bulletless gun. "Where is your weapon?"

Markus tapped the pocket of his jacket.

"How many bullets do you have?"

"Two."

"Two bullets?" Vladimir said. "That's all?"

"I bought this gun because of you," Markus said. "I only ever thought I would need two bullets. One to wound you and the other to deliver the kill shot."

Vladimir's mouth opened wide. He had no time to imagine an alternate reality in which he might have stormed into Markus's office, knife in hand, hiccupping with a deranged look in his eyes and met the barrel of Markus's gun full on. He tucked his empty Nagant revolver into his jacket.

"How many guards are watching over Doctor Namestikov right now?"

"Three, I believe," Ilvana said. "As far as I know, the execution squad isn't scheduled to arrive until eleven. After that, there won't be much time."

"Three guards we can handle," Vladimir said, as though the men watching over Sergei were an abstract concept and not real men with muscles and strength and determination.

"But we only have two bullets." Markus pointed his cane in the air. "And I don't intend on murdering anyone tonight. I want to make that perfectly clear."

"We won't have to shoot anyone. We'll just use the threat of force. Ilvana can get us into the hospital. I'll threaten the guards and Markus can gather the doctor. We'll be in and out before they know what happened."

"What will we do afterward? Where will we go? Where will Sergei live?" Markus said.

Vladimir paused. He hadn't considered any of this. Was it really feasible to take Sergei back to his village to live with him and his mother? How would they traverse the frozen river? What would they do for food and money along the way? A hairline crack formed in the enameled surface of Vladimir's conviction.

"I can't answer those questions now," he said. He pointed at the clock on the wall. "We have less than forty minutes to save our friend." Vladimir walked toward the door. "Which of you has the courage to come with me?"

twenty-three

"Where's your driver?" Vladimir said.

Markus walked around to the back of his car and looked down the street. He peered this way and that, the freezing rain blowing sideways in the wind, looked back at Vladimir and Ilvana and then up at the building across the street, where a few illuminated windows were scattered like missing puzzle pieces. He lifted his cane and pointed. "Up there, I presume."

"You said he was on duty."

"He is. At least he's supposed to be," Markus said.

"Then what's he doing up there?"

Markus wagged his finger in the air. He spoke directly to the building. "That little street-corner strumpet finally tricked you into her lair, didn't she? You should be ashamed of yourself, Nikolai. You're a married man. You have two children. Have you no shame? Have you no sense of decency?" He turned to Vladimir. "I have half a mind to go up there right now and catch him in the act."

"We don't have time for that," Vladimir said. "Can you drive the car yourself?"

Markus shook his head. "I haven't got a license."

"That doesn't matter. Do you know how to drive?"

"Of course I understand the principles of operating a moving vehicle," Markus said. "But my legs are too short to reach the pedals and I'm barely strong enough to turn the wheel."

Vladimir turned to Ilvana. She was slumped against the

driver's-side door, her eyes closed, soft intermittent wisps of air seeping through her lips. There was no way Vladimir could let her drive. She would fall asleep as she turned a corner and kill them all.

"What about you?" Markus said.

"I've never driven a car."

"Never?"

"That's what I said, isn't it?" Vladimir snapped in anger. He was growing frustrated. Time was passing too quickly. They were only five kilometers from the hospital but they might as well have been on the other side of the world. "Fine," he said. "I'll drive and you'll instruct me."

Vladimir placed Ilvana in the backseat and helped Markus into the passenger's side. Markus stood straight up on his two feet, his hair barely brushing against the ceiling as he instructed Vladimir on the necessary fundamentals. He told Vladimir which pedal was for acceleration and which operated the brakes. He offered advice on the amount of force required to steer the car from side to side and insisted on helping with the shifting. Vladimir placed his hands on the wheel. He moved his foot from the clutch to the brake and then to the gas and back again. He turned the key in the ignition and the car revved to a start. It hopped forward. Markus bellowed instructions in Vladimir's ear. Vladimir's hands gripped tighter on the wheel. The car hopped forward as Markus shifted the vehicle directly into third gear. Vladimir pressed on the gas and they were off. A smile tickled the corners of Vladimir's mouth. Even in his frantic, disoriented state, the adrenaline rushed through his veins. He turned the car to the left and they lurched down the road with Ilvana asleep in the back. Vladimir yelled out. "Woo!" he screamed again and stepped on the gas.

When it came time to turn right, Vladimir placed his foot

down again. Suddenly the car sped up instead of slowing down. Vladimir didn't know what to do. He pressed down even harder, but in his euphoric state he'd confused the brake pedal and the gas. The car shot through the streets like an out-of-control barrel of apples rolling down a hill. Markus screamed in his native British. Another car — the only other automobile on the road — was directly ahead. Vladimir searched valiantly for the brake with his foot but found the clutch instead. The engine made a hideous gasping noise.

Crash!

The car came to a stop with its front end firmly embedded in the back end of the other vehicle. An enraged man, big and burly, stepped out of the other car, cursing under his breath. Vladimir glanced at his wristwatch. Very little time remained.

"Hand me your gun," he said.

"I most certainly will not," Markus said. "What do you plan to do with it?"

Ilvana had woken up with the crash and was talking nonsense in Vladimir's ear.

The other driver, still fuming, was approaching.

"Hand me your gun," Vladimir said again, calmly and directly.

This time Markus relented. He reached inside his jacket and handed Vladimir the weapon. Vladimir stepped out of the car. He pointed the gun at the other driver.

"You best be on your way," Vladimir said.

The other driver froze in place. He stared into the barrel of the gun with a petrified expression on his face. Vladimir raised the weapon in the air and fired a single shot. It was louder than he'd imagined, the force of the gun stronger too. The weapon kicked back in Vladimir's hand. He gripped the handle tighter and took aim once more.

"I only have one bullet left," he said to the speechless motorist. "Don't make me feel like I need to use it."

The man nodded his head. He apologized and turned around and climbed into his vehicle. At first when he pressed on the gas, his car wouldn't budge, its back end was so firmly entrenched in the pile of gears and metal. He accelerated harder. His tires skidded in the sleet and then found traction on the pavement. The two vehicles pulled apart with a loud metallic screech. Off down the road the other car hobbled. Vladimir watched it disappear into the Russian night.

He tossed the gun back to Markus.

Markus's eyes turned wild as the weapon sailed through the air and he let out a shriek before catching it in his hands. "Terrific," he said. "Now we only have one bullet left."

Vladimir walked to the front of the car to survey the damage. It looked bad, without a doubt. But it still appeared drivable. The car would get them the short distance they had to travel. He looked back at Markus and Ilvana.

In the distance, sirens sounded. Fast-approaching headlights peppered the horizon.

"We need to work out another arrangement," he said. "And quickly."

Markus took a step toward Ilvana. "Do you know how to drive?"

She hesitated.

"My father stopped me from driving when I was eighteen."

"What happened when you were eighteen?" Vladimir said.

"Yes, what happened?" Markus said.

"I hit a sheep."

"That's not so bad," Markus said.

"And a couple of dogs. But they were only strays. Not a single collar was found in the wreckage."

"Well . . ."

"Also my grandmother's wheelchair."

"Oh."

"*Babooshka* was in the chair at the time," Ilvana said. "When the car struck, it made an awful sound. I've never quite forgotten it."

Ilvana looked to be on the verge of weeping. Vladimir gazed off into the distance. For the first time, an orange-red glow appeared along the horizon. The Germans were advancing. The world was on fire — Moscow might burn to the ground tonight — and Vladimir's doctor was scheduled to die in mere minutes. He looked at the deserted city streets. There wasn't a single stray animal or disabled grandmother in sight.

"We'll have to make do," he said.

The trio arrived at the hospital gates eight minutes later with Vladimir in the passenger seat and Ilvana driving the car. Markus was sitting square on her lap, helping her steer. He'd propped her chin up with his piecemeal coif of hair, and whenever Ilvana's concentration started to wane, Vladimir would holler in her ear and Markus would knock her straight on the chin with the back of his head. As they approached the hospital gates, Vladimir saw the same military personnel carrying large guns that he'd seen earlier in the day. Ilvana pulled the car up next to them and Vladimir thought they were doomed for sure. The soldiers would take one look at the car's smashed front end still steaming in the rain, one look at the narcoleptic nurse's aide driving with a malformed troll

— a foreigner, no less — sitting in her lap and arrest them all on the spot.

Vladimir was shocked to see Ilvana exchange pleasantries with the guards. They appeared to know each other, or at the very least to have spoken before as Ilvana commented on the cold night and made a joke about teaching her diminutive friend to drive. The soldiers hardly listened to her, preoccupied as they were with staring at the orange glow of war pulsing in the distance. They told Ilvana to hurry on her way, and then stepped back to let the car pass.

"Well done!" Markus said once they were out of earshot.

"What now?" Vladimir said.

Ilvana pulled the vehicle around to the side of the building that occupied the mental health ward and parked it against a wall. They stepped out and stood in the rain. It was ten minutes until eleven. Ten minutes until the execution.

"Now we go get your doctor."

twenty-four

The moment Ilvana inserted her key and opened the door, Vladimir wilted. He could keep himself together no longer. Plagued by terrors since the moment his hiccups stopped, he placed one foot inside the building and felt like he was about to die. The smell was incredible, incurable, inerasable. It wafted toward him. Like humid summer heat, it seeped into his mouth, penetrated his eyes and permeated his every pore. Screams sounded in the distance with the deranged, the retarded and the sick all calling out into the dark. Imprisoned in these bloodstained walls as much as in their fragile minds, their voices comingled to form one long, inescapable moan. Two steps inside the building, Vladimir grasped a handrail on the stairwell. For the first time in his life, he prayed, he prayed to die here, for the dark to overtake him, to not have to walk these halls again.

Markus dropped his cane and grabbed Vladimir's hand. He helped him up a single stair and then another. Ilvana assisted as well. Inside Vladimir's brain, angry ravens pecked at his cerebellum. He didn't know who he was, who he'd been, what he was doing here anymore. The three of them kept climbing stairs until they reached another door. Ilvana pulled a second set of keys from her pocket. They bridged the precipice and entered a giant hall where the lunatics walked freely. Some crept along the floor like animals. Others shuffled their feet and dragged their invisible chains. That night Vladimir spent here all those years ago rushed to the front of his brain. He remembered that first moonstruck schizophrenic who attacked him with a garbage can, the wild brawl that escalated amongst the patients and staff, the fire, the carnage, the beheaded nurse. It all made the trial in the Waterfall of Ion seem like a leisurely bath.

Ilvana and Markus tried to hurry Vladimir along. An old woman, naked from the waist up, grasped at him.

"Hurry, Vladimir. You must move your feet!"

It was Ilvana's voice. Vladimir looked over at her. How awake she appeared now, how in and of the moment. Vladimir pulled his arm away from the naked woman and kept moving forward. Where were his hiccups? Where was the pressing urge, the hourglass steadily dripping sand that had come to define his life? Together Vladimir, Markus and Ilvana pushed past the unoccupied nurses' station and through another set of doors. Vladimir recognized this hallway. It was white and windowless like all the others, and he knew it from the uneven number of doorways on either side. The last time he was here, bodies had littered the floor. *Where are they now?* he wondered. *What became of those lost souls?*

Ilvana approached a third and final door. To Vladimir's surprise, Markus already had his pistol drawn, his tiny partial thumb and malformed fingers coiled around the trigger. The door opened and there was Sergei, standing alone, chains around his wrists and ankles.

Markus burst into the room brandishing his weapon with more bravado than Vladimir believed possible. He pointed his gun into all four corners, twirled around, looked at his old friend and then back at Ilvana.

"Where are the guards?" he said.

Ilvana stole a glance back in the hallway. She gave Markus a confused look.

"Vladimir? Markus? Is it really you?" Sergei said.

He was standing in the center of the room, stark naked, his frail bones bulging through his skin. Blue iridescent veins formed spiderwebs on his flesh. Death's door was upon him and his eyes flickered, twitching and convulsing with each sideways glance. He looked like he hadn't eaten since Vladimir last saw him. And his hiccups — the ones he'd feigned all along — were gone.

"You've come to kill me, haven't you?" he said.

Markus lowered his gun. "Of course not, old friend. We've come to save you."

"They're coming right now." Sergei glanced at the open doorway behind him. "The guards took my clothes and left. They told me to wait here for the executioner's axe." He shuffled along the floor toward Markus. "I hope they don't use an axe," he said. "The very thought of it turns my fingers numb. I can't feel. I can't think. I'm not myself anymore."

"You needn't worry, old friend," Markus said. "We're here to save you." He reached out to grasp Sergei's hand when Vladimir fell to the floor and started to scream.

"I can't take it anymore!" Vladimir yelled. He crawled on his knees toward Sergei. "Please, I beg of you. Make my hiccups come back. Return me to the man I used to be. I can't take this noise, this noise, noise, noise! This place, these people, this world — it never ends. It just keeps on ticking like a broken clock. Help me. You're the only one who can save me!"

Sergei stepped back. He looked down at his naked body and the chains around his wrists and ankles. Behind him footsteps thundered down the hall. They were coming. "I can't save you, my son, any more than you can save me," Sergei said.

The footsteps stopped and at the doorway appeared three

figures — two tall, muscular men in suits and a short, older man with wide innocent eyes and a serious expression across his face. He carried in his hand a large axe.

"Stop right where you are." Markus held his gun in the air. "We're leaving with this man and there's nothing you can do to stop us."

Vladimir was in tears now. He could barely breathe.

"Afin?" Sergei said.

The executioner looked the doctor Namestikov square in the eyes. He took two steps forward, axe in hand. "Sergei?" he whispered.

One of the men in suits tapped Sergei's former driver on the shoulder. "Do you know this man?"

"Of course," he said. "He's a doctor. His opinion is held in the highest esteem in the medical community."

"Then why is he naked? Why is he wearing chains?"

Afin and Sergei shared a long knowing glare while Markus and the two men in suits stared each other down. Vladimir was struggling to climb to his feet. Ilvana, the poor thing, had fallen asleep in the corridor.

"The midget did it!" Afin said suddenly. He pointed at Markus holding his gun. "He must have caught the good doctor off guard and fastened him in chains."

"Then who are we here to execute?" the man in the suit said.

Afin pointed his finger at Vladimir, who was standing on shaky legs. "Him! He's the one. That's Sergei Namestikov."

Markus screamed a vigorous objection, but before it could exit his windpipe, Afin swung the butt end of his axe straight into Markus's nose. Blood shot out in black clumps. Markus faltered and dropped his cane. The gun with its single bullet fell to the ground.

"That's right!" Sergei screamed. He too pointed at Vladimir.

"He's the one who killed that bastard Alexander! Execute him! Not me!"

The two men in suits exchanged confused glances. Vladimir looked over at Sergei jumping wildly, his chains clanking against the ground. Vladimir's mind raced. He felt both dead and alive, bewildered and betrayed. He stumbled toward the doctor.

"Why?" he said.

Sergei stopped jumping and placed his mouth to Vladimir's ear. "All men betray, Vladimir. All men fail one another. I can't go into the black void not knowing what's there for me. I'm too weak. My conviction is too frail. I'm sorry, my boy. I'm not the man I used to be."

Sergei pushed Vladimir away. Their eyes met, they converged, and Vladimir knew now that what he'd long hoped — that he and his doctor were two different versions of the same man, opposite sides of a coin, brothers, father and son, likened souls on this earthly plain — was simply not true.

Sergei's eyes drifted away and then turned wild again. He jumped up and down and pointed. "Kill him! He's the one you want. Kill him quickly before he kills you!"

The shock of his doctor's betrayal caused a jolt deep inside Vladimir. He stepped back. A sensation triggered in his chest, one so strange and yet familiar that he couldn't quite believe it was happening. He swallowed three swift gulps of air. A flicker echoed in the back of his throat.

By the doorway, the men in suits engaged in a brief consultation. Markus tried to object, tried to stand up, but his legs failed him and his mouth had filled with blood. Ilvana was still asleep in the corridor.

"Are you absolutely sure about this?" the man in the suit said to Afin.

"I've never been more positive about anything in my whole life." Afin pointed to Vladimir. "I was given a photograph of that young man just last night. He's the one who killed Alexander Afiniganov. He's Sergei Namestikov."

The man nodded. "Okay, let's get this over with."

Vladimir was waiting — not for the executioner and his minions to edge toward him, but for the hourglass to tip over again and bleed sand, for the world to resume spinning on its axis.

He could feel it at the back of his tongue now, through his rib cage even.

Afin and his goons approached. Six hands reached toward him. Vladimir tried to push them away. He could hear Sergei in the background, naked and in chains, jumping eagerly and screaming out directions. He tried to reach into his jacket and get out his empty gun, to pistol-whip them all into submission. But they were too many. The malaise in his mind was too strong. He felt their hands on his shoulders, felt himself being pushed to his knees.

His chest contorted, Vladimir's phrenic nerve contracted involuntarily.

Then it happened. Finally.

Hiccup.

That rhythm returned, that constant knowing, the realization that the world was a place he could understand and feel and touch and know. Vladimir took it all in, the dim light in this lost room, the dense air against his skin. He breathed in and waited in anticipation for the next convulsive yelp.

In the corner, Sergei stopped jumping. Vladimir's hiccup, that sound he'd become accustomed to so long ago, entered through his ear canal, danced along his tympanic membrane and reverberated inside his ear like a soft brush whispering against a drum. He looked at Vladimir, his patient, his son. The evil men had forced Vladimir to the ground. Sergei saw not a grown man, but that helpless little boy from long ago. Years earlier he'd held Vladimir's hand while his young charge drifted off to sleep. He'd nurtured the boy, read to him by candlelight stories from colorful picture books, brushed the hair from Vladimir's forehead, cared for him, loved him as a father would.

What has Alexander done to me, Sergei thought, *that I have become such a monster?*

Afin was struggling to place a shroud over Vladimir's head.

"No!" Sergei screamed. He jumped forward and grabbed hold of Afin's arm. "I'm the real Sergei Namestikov," he yelled. "Take me! Kill me! Spare the boy."

Afin looked at him now like he was truly mad. He tossed Sergei's weakened body aside as though it were a pillowcase stuffed with feathers.

"Vladimir!" Sergei lunged again. This time he took hold of his young charge's hand. "Forgive me," he said. "Forgive all that I have done. I'm sorry. I love you. I never meant to put you in harm's way."

Vladimir took Sergei's hand in his. Afin's assistants paused with their hands still on Vladimir's shoulders. They looked back at Afin, waiting for instructions.

Vladimir released another hiccup, this one glorious and defiant. He felt like a patient on a gurney, given up for dead only to have had his heart miraculously start beating once more. He was himself again. Sergei had come back to save him, just as Vladimir had done for his beloved doctor. Vladimir warbled out a smile. Sergei was still a good man. The world had not torn him apart after all.

He knew what he had to do.

"I am Sergei Namestikov," Vladimir said.

"No!" Sergei yelled.

"I killed Alexander Afiniganov," Vladimir said. "And I am to be put to death."

Afin's assistants looked at Afin in confusion again. Afin pulled Sergei away from Vladimir, and when Sergei struggled, he clubbed the doctor in the nose, the same as Markus. Sergei reeled. Blood shot forth from his mouth and he collapsed in the corner. Afin's assistants returned to positioning Vladimir, only with increased determination.

It happened so quickly. The executioner wrapped the shroud over Vladimir's head. Everything turned dark and suddenly the world disappeared. The Earth, these evildoers, the sun and the trees outside, this room, all of Russia left him.

Vladimir allowed his body to go loose. He thought of Ileana, her pretty eyes, how peaceful she looked sitting in the snow. He thought of his mother's smile as they ate boiled cabbage at the kitchen table, the farmer's daughter naked and serene in the moonlight.

The axe cut through the air.

Hiccup.

There it was again. Was it enough? Had the world turned out to be the place Vladimir imagined it to be? Was it just and fair, made of roses and rainbows and butterflies, or was it evil and depraved, a purgatory of untold suffering? Perhaps a bit of both.

The darkness approached. Vladimir basked in that last hiccup. The axe hurtled down toward him. Was there one more to come? He felt it in his chest, in his shoulders, in his soul. What more could he have done with his life than know something to be true, than hold on to it with all his power? What more could Vladimir have done than die trying to save the man who tried to save him all those years ago? Was God waiting for him on the other side? Were his ancestors? Were the drowned and the decapitated and the burned alive dancing for joy in the next realm? What more could there be than just this world?

Hiccup.

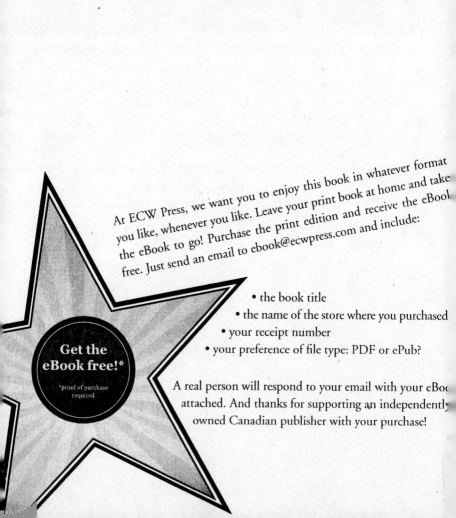

At ECW Press, we want you to enjoy this book in whatever format you like, whenever you like. Leave your print book at home and take the eBook to go! Purchase the print edition and receive the eBook free. Just send an email to ebook@ecwpress.com and include:

- the book title
- the name of the store where you purchased
- your receipt number
- your preference of file type: PDF or ePub?

A real person will respond to your email with your eBook attached. And thanks for supporting an independently owned Canadian publisher with your purchase!

Get the eBook free!*

*proof of purchase required